# Dreaming .400

# Praise for Dreaming .400

"Eleven baseball-related short stories—delightfully off-center—the author in search of some exotic Balm of Gilead that might make all things right. Myers' stories remind me of W. P. Kinsella's fanciful approach to the game, where the natural and mystical walk hand-in-hand.  He tells his stories in a voice that is all his own, unique even as it reflects the spirit of baseball flowing across the years."

**Bill Young, co-author, *Remembering the Montreal Expos* and *Ecstasy to Agony: The 1994 Montreal Expos***

"Great collection of stories. They reminded me of the days when I first discovered baseball—the pickup games, a taped-up bat, afternoons at the schoolyard, and hanging out with friends. So many unique characters here and so many ways baseball impacted their lives. Anyone who loves the game and original storytelling will enjoy DREAMING .400."

**Craig Counsell, Manager, Milwaukee Brewers**

"In Steve Myers' Dreaming .400, you have the next generation of short story matriculation, W. P. Kinsella's "Thrill of the Grass," T. C. Boyle out of USC...Carry the mantle proudly, Steve Myers. You gravitate to the right metaphor about baseball--all the different kinds of people.  You and [Hillel] Wright and Kinsella are the only ones writing short stories like this today."

**Bill "Spaceman" Lee**

"What is it about writers and baseball? What makes writers/baseball fans such acute observers of character? Perhaps we should ask Steve Myers, he's one of those guys. Or perhaps not: The man's too much of a natural to explain this stuff."

**Marc Robitaille – screenwriter, co-author of *Il Était Une Fois les Expos***

# Dreaming .400

## Tales of Baseball Redemption

Steve Myers

ISBN: 978-1-938545-64-1 (print)
ISBN: 978-1-938545-65-8 (ebook)

For information about permissions, bulk purchases,
or additional distribution, write to

Summer Game Books
P. O. Box 818
South Orange, NJ 07079
or contact the publisher at
www.summergamebooks.com

Cover painting, "Illuminating the Joe,"
by Judy McSween

To Sarah: For listening,

listening some more,

and then speaking her mind

# Acknowledgments

Walter Friedman and Summer Game Books.
Bill Young.
Pen pals through the years.
Sarah.
Mom, Dad, and brother Mike.

# About the Author

Steve Myers grew up in Milwaukee and has been a Brewers fan for as long as he can remember, but it was Cleveland Indian's pitcher Bert Blyleven that shocked him into a universe of endless baseball lore.

Steve was 13 when he poked his head into the Indians dugout and asked, "Can I have your autograph Mr. Blyleven?" Neil Heaton approached instead and distracted him so Blyleven could set Steve's shoelace on fire. The boy had been hotfooted. He also received an autographed baseball.

Steve collected baseball cards, pursued a broadcasting career in his living room, and played a solid left field for his high school team.

He studied history at the University of Wisconsin-Milwaukee and graduated with honors. It was James Liddy's Beat Literature class, however, that jumpstarted Steve's poetry and wanderlust. He studied in southern Spain, lived in San Francisco and Brooklyn, and for the last 13 years Montreal, Quebec where he witnessed the end of Expos baseball.

Steve recently earned a graduate diploma in journalism from Montreal's Concordia University. He has published articles on a variety of topics, from university baseball to the Native American naming of streets. He is the author of the blog, *Brewers Baseball and Things.*

# Contents

# Dear Reader

A red whiffle ball bat in my hands felt like a cave man club. The barrel was so fat. Dad said I hit everything in sight! No wonder I got hooked. There was security in stacks of baseball cards. I put up a Joe Charboneau poster. Strat-o-matic became a Friday night pastime. I loved going to County Stadium. Harold Baines was my hero.

All the tidbits and trivia, the games and players, the books and stories, stadiums and even the scandals are like an endless flea market to me and I return there often. It's where I create characters and plots and weave them into the past. It's where fact and fiction dance and Dreaming .400 comes to life.

"Illuminating the Joe" by Judy McSween is the title of *Dreaming .400's* cover art. The stadium's official name is Joseph P. Riley Jr. Park, in Charleston, South Carolina, home to the Class A RiverDogs of the South Atlantic League.

Somewhere in "The Joe" a scorecard is being filled out. A number sets sail from the page, floats up like steam and transforms into a letter, then a word and a sentence and a story, maybe barnstorming by canoe, from backwoods country fields to urban junk yards. Why not?

Enjoy dreaming .400. Thanks for reading.

Steve Myers

Montreal, Canada

August, 2015

# Season of the Pitch

It was tempting to dabble in astrology when Kerri Shipling walked across the baseball diamond and took the mound because we weren't really sure if she was a he.

Gemini was our obvious choice. She didn't pitch ambidextrous like Greg Harris, but a future of dragging fold up coffee tables up and down big city avenues with tarot cards tucked in urban vests flashed through our minds anyway.

The corner positions settled on airplane manufacturing and rivets. The shortstop opened up a nightclub. But the second baseman messed around with palm readings and numerology, mostly predicting the outcomes of sporting events. I say "but" because soothsayers of any kind always fascinated us outfielders. We jumped around from job to job.

Kerri appeared to us when days were free-flowing and no one cared about decimal points and sounding smart. Only the catcher was a scientist. He had no choice. The ninja equipment and flashing signs did him in. The rest of us lumped everything together and called it wind. It was easier that way.

There were fewer complications, just moments and wind, here today and gone tomorrow. Gender bending was water switching states, more of the same, here today and gone tomorrow. We didn't care if you were a boy or a girl. Just throw the ball, and a few years later, toss a beer back. Blow the harmonica. Sing. Make your own noise.

There were years, if not decades, to pick up bad habits, and we did our best every damn day without really knowing how much we might need the memories. But the rewards were immediate as well. At night we laughed about ripping off Old Man Bear and his dirty pharmacy or knocking over real estate signs on green lawns.

Kerri Shipling painted corners with strikes, but that was only half of it. She could lay down a drag bunt with Minnesota Fats precision, as perfect as Rod Carew and people pegged her a "Charlie Hustle type," but only until witnessing one of her line drive whistles that rolled all the way to the outfield wall. Then they shut up.

Kerri set fire to people's notions without even trying. I remember the poster of Gary Mathews on her bedroom wall, "The Sarge." He began with the Giants, then the Braves and Phillies, but we enjoyed him as a Chicago Cub twitching in the batter's box with wrist bands jacked up to his forearm, coolest player in the universe.

Kerri introduced me to kids I might have never met on my own, rough kids who smoked joints and had older brothers in prison. Kerry could read the pulse of anyone, including that skinny kid always wearing turtle necks.

He wasn't much of a baseball player or didn't look like one anyway. He weighed less than 100 pounds and stood five feet ten inches. It was painful to watch, because on a windy day, we joked, he might end up in the next town.

He looked more like a prisoner of war than a ballplayer, but it was his eyes that really bothered us. They didn't move. He could stare at you for more than two minutes without blinking. If that doesn't seem like very long—try it sometime. Most of us lasted no more than 40 seconds before thinking about our mothers.

He became the object of our taunts, but no one actually hit him, just fake punches and name calling, mostly "freak" and "weirdo" with a few "wing nuts" thrown in. But nothing bothered the kid. It was like he couldn't hear or see anyone.

Landing Powell was his name, but we all called him "Ding" for short. We had no choice. We were too upset to call him by his birth name because most of us so-called baseball players dreamed of having a name like Landing Powell, so powerful and out of this world, a Babe Ruth sort of name, but whatever power we attached to it quickly disappeared when Ding stepped to the plate or ran out to a position at Matchbox Field.

He couldn't hit and could barely keep the mitt on his hand. He looked like a puppet running down the first base line, strings for arms and legs flailing all over the place. But there was no denying what happened one Saturday during the only season Ding ever played.

It was the second game of the day so players from the first game were still hanging around and players for the third game were warming up. The people traffic was thickest during that middle game, with parents, players, kid brothers and sisters loitering around, and this may sound crazy or downright impossible, but I could hear the noise in people's brains come to a screeching stop when Ding did it.

The dimensions at Matchbox Field had been expanded in the off season to 250 feet down the lines, 275 to dead center, with the outfield alleys somewhere in between. Foul poles were also installed. No one expected anyone to hit a home run, and up until that Saturday when Ding went deep, no one had, not even Bill Blitzkoff, the previous season's league leader with 15 when the fences were much closer in.

Ding showed no emotion when Coach Middleton embraced him, and even less when his father trespassed into the dugout, arriving a few seconds after the home run. Ding's dad didn't say a word. He just bowed in the direction of home plate and returned to his seat, never even congratulated his son, never even looked at him.

Kerri was the only one who took an interest in Ding. The two of them sat at the end of the dugout talking. We caught snippets of their conversations through the fence when one of them walked to the on-deck circle. They talked about rabbit's feet and frying ants with a magnifying glass, how to grow spices in pickle buckets and other things no one really cared about. We listened anyway because Kerri didn't stay very long in any particular place, but she planted seeds wherever she went and we didn't want to miss anything.

We became convinced she had willed Ding's home run, not in some Marvel Comics super hero sort of way, but none of us would put it past her, either.

Ding's home run cleared the fence in right center field with plenty of room to spare. We calculated it at 300 feet. An opposite field blast like that was extremely rare for a 12-year old, especially a kid with no skill and no interest in baseball whatsoever.

Players wasted away hours in batting cages and learned how to go with an outside pitch, drive it to the opposite field. If you were a right-handed batter, a line drive over the second baseman's head was a thing of beauty and a one hopper to the wall in right center bordered on greatness, so an opposite field home run hit by a right-handed wing nut freak made us wonder about rain dances and magic potions.

Maybe if Ding had kept playing, we wouldn't have cared so much. We could have seen him swing and miss dozens of times and stopped feeling so envious of him, but he joined the school band immediately after hitting that home run, played the tuba or trombone, practiced on his front porch so everyone could hear. It made us nervous. We called Ding new names like "brass bastard," but nothing changed. It was still like he couldn't hear or see anyone.

We asked Kerri if she would speak to Ding's parents and try and change their minds. We couldn't afford to have him quit baseball while on top. We needed to see him fail. Our own futures depended on it. The home run played in our heads over and over and over.

"Change their minds to what?" Kerri asked. "Maybe he's the one who doesn't want to play."

Kerri was wise beyond her years. The rest of us weren't and so we refused to accept that a 12-year old could sync his hips and wrists like that and extend his arms and blast such a long home run. It wasn't fair, not by a kid who one week earlier held a bat like it was a wet noodle. Ding had already achieved what we all coveted, an out of the park, out of this world home run. How could he just walk away from it all?

We could all hit, but only the lucky few like Ding could stop and stare at a ball they had sent into orbit. Only they could take their sweet old time. The rest of us had to be industrious and hard working. We had to "run it out" no matter what, even after an embarrassing infield pop. "Run it out!"

But not the sultans of swat like Landing Powell. They could fling the bat aside like a stripper does her top. They could gallop or trot, or if they were feeling real perverse and cocky, they could drop their arm into a make-believe holster and impersonate Jeffrey Leonard's one flap down. They could snort any old way they liked, and in the process, waft their own unique smell everywhere.

It was animal and primal and as Kerry always said, "An electricity lingering till your dying days," and well, that just made it worse for the rest of us, like we were somehow incomplete, like the animal side of our nature was stuck in captivity and we had failed to free it.

Hard to believe that some people, especially the Punch-and-Judy types, mocked the home run, called it "nothing special," preferring the industry of a manufactured run. *The home run, they said, lacks the subtlety of the game's greater achievements—the hit and run or stolen base, suicide squeeze.*

Blah, blah, blah. We knew their banter as a disguise. They were jealous. It became crystal clear when our cleanup hitter, Bill Blitzkoff, hit one a country mile. These same soon-to-be-scholarly dweebs preaching about bunts and stolen bases were the ones jumping up and down and suddenly in awe of the home run because we had the lead and would be enjoying a free ice cream if that lead stuck.

Kerri never talked to Ding's parents, but she never stopped talking to Ding either, only their venue changed, from the end of the dugout bench to Ding's patio where he played the tuba or trombone. Kerri didn't care that Ding was no longer interested in baseball. He wanted to play music and that was fine with Kerri, but not with us.

We asked Kerri to invite Ding to the field. It didn't have to be an official game and it didn't matter who pitched.

Kerri thought it was a great idea and so did Ding. Took most of us by surprise. We expected Ding to say no because he never really seemed to care about baseball. But the opposite happened. The two of them were on the diamond the next morning and every morning for an entire week.

They would meet beyond the right field home run fence, in the very spot where Ding hit his home run. They were nothing but two silhouettes out there, so we sent a few players on spy missions to find out what Kerri was telling Ding. The spies were our kid brothers so they did what we asked or lost their lunch money.

They returned with short fragments of conversation like "More than one way to hit a baseball." It wasn't enough so we had them follow Kerri and Ding to the library where they managed to get the names of books left behind on tables.

They were mostly baseball books, one about stadium architecture, another on the Brooklyn Excelsiors, but also two books about Poseidon, and one coffee table colorful book about Zuni Fetishes.

It made sense, because the following afternoon the spies returned with more snippets from Kerri's conversation that sounded kind of Zuni-like, "every hitter is different, each with an animal spirit buried within."

Kerri insisted the game be played Saturday night after all the other games were completed and all the fans and coaches and scorekeepers had gone home.

"What are you talking about Kerri?" someone asked. "There are no lights at Matchbox Field. Will we be playing in the dark?"

Everyone laughed, but Kerri insisted. "Just be there after sundown. Meet in the woods beyond right field and trust me, you'll see just fine."

Some came because they were curious, but most of us came to witness a weakness so we could trap it and preserve it in our memories for the rest of our lives. Landing Powell was going down. He had to.

We arrived with flashlights, but Kerri asked us to shut them off, so we did. It was so dark we couldn't even see each other.

We missed that scary-looking water tower with its dome top and prison bars and the way it dripped cold water pearls into the wind and onto our bare arms and faces, and during the day sent shadows across the infield. It was kind of creepy, but at least it was familiar. We were hoping a train might chug along the grassy slope beyond left field. It would be good to see boxcars fill up the horizon like an accordion. We needed something, anything. It was dark. We were scared.

Kerri called on the sky or moon or stars in some language none of us had ever heard. The field didn't light up like a sunny day. It was more like night vision, but we could see clearer than a Saturday afternoon. We ran out to our positions without saying a word.

Kerri offered the pitcher's mound to anyone interested, but we all trusted her or were mesmerized by her, the way she moved like a jellyfish in slow, syncopated thrusts and glides like she was underwater or something, pulsating.

Ding stood at the plate, still looking sickly and skinny, but very relaxed, or maybe he just didn't care. He held the bat real low at his side with the tip almost pointing towards the ground. Kerri stood out there for a good two minutes. The two of them stared at each other like a pitcher and catcher sometimes do, with heads completely still.

The first pitch was a fastball that appeared to be heading for Ding's ribs, but he stepped to his left and swiveled his hips in perfect sync with his swing. We didn't see the ball, but we heard the twang of the aluminum bat followed by a long pause and then the rustle of grass and knew it could only have landed in one place, on the hilly slope, beside the railroad tracks in left field.

Ding didn't move, didn't say a thing. Neither did any of us. We were all in shock, in part because Ding had done it again and also because we were able to hear a ball flapping through a thicket of grass more than 300 feet away.

We all walked home without saying a word. That was the last time Ding played baseball and the last time Kerri mentioned the two in the same breath. From then on it was just Ding and his music. The taunting and name calling stopped and most of us began listening to Ding play tuba. It was definitely a tuba and not a trombone. He wasn't half bad either.

Landing Powell had hit not one, but two home runs and we never discovered how Kerri Shipling helped him do it, and as it turned out, we needed the memory of not knowing more than we could have ever imagined.

# To Be Frank

Frank Moreno visited Colorado, California and Texas. He rode his bike through Ohio and West Virginia, attended Cubs games in Illinois, was born in South Dakota, moved to Wisconsin, and there were many more states. There were nation states and chemical states and every once in a while drunken states, but there were never any states quite like the sizzle state, not for Frank anyway.

It happened anywhere and anytime. There were no metal detectors to walk through, no borders to cross. It could be while waiting in one of those long lines at the post office. People begin to sigh and blow grumpy from their nostrils, but not Frank.

*He thinks of it as mountains or alligator-infested rivers and*
*suddenly a pigeon launches from the window ledge*
*and the entire concept of mail hijacks Frank.*
*the stamps and sorting and*
*over-the-road trucks, airplanes, diesel smell,*
*continental divide and on the other side,*
*more over the road trucks and more sorting,*
*a strange shaped mail delivery truck,*
*a mailman dressed in blue,*
*some delivery on feet and sound of clink,*
*as life inside houses and apartments stirs.*

*Presto abracadabra...*
*Frank Moreno is next in line.*

Frank grew up on his father's potato farm in Oacoma, South Dakota, beside the Missouri River, within an ear shot of Interstate 90 and the hissing of trucks. Frank learned how to walk and talk and go the bathroom in a toilet. Life was good in South Dakota.

Sal Moreno was Frank's father. One day, he moved his family east along that same Interstate 90, all the way to New Berlin, Wisconsin. Frank and his brother and two sisters packed up their belongings in boxes. A moving company took care of the rest.

New Berlin is a 15-minute bus ride from Milwaukee. Frank delivered *Milwaukee Journal* newspapers every afternoon, except Sunday because on Sunday the *Journal* was a morning paper.

Frank wore a saddle bag and walked up and down long driveways and bushy backyards delivering those papers. He was determined to save enough money so he could join the Milwaukee Brewers' Pepsi Fan Club. Delivery in all kinds of weather proved to be a great challenge, but Frank wrote his first poem as a tribute to Milwaukee winters:

### How to walk in snow

*each step a rocky mountain,*
*3-feet deep in impossible dreams*
*that instantly come true.*

*each step a rocky mountain,*
*3-feet deep in impossible dreams*
*that instantly come true.*

*repeat*

*repeat*

*repeat*

Frank wasn't too interested in video game arcades or cute girls so he had no problem saving money for a fan club membership. He was 15 years young and had a baseball team to root for, a place to watch them play – County Stadium – and a father willing to be his escort. Frank Moreno was living a dream.

County Stadium was located at the bottom of the Menominee Valley. Frank liked the name Menominee. It was exotic sounding and so were the names Milwaukee and Kinnickinnic, and all three were local rivers emptying into Lake Michigan.

The Pepsi Fan Club starter kit included a mesh trucker snapback cap, an official major league baseball, Pepsi Fan Club identification card, a 10 percent discount on all Brewers merchandise, and most importantly, tickets to 10 home games. The seats were always on the first base Brewers home dugout side, lower grandstand, about 20-25 rows up. Frank loved to talk while watching the game.

"I hope the new stadiums are big like they used to be," Frank would say, "So the baseball has some place to roll, so there will be more and more triples. I love triples."

"What new stadiums?" a fellow fan club member would ask.

"They always build new stadiums," replied Frank. "Do you think County Stadium grew on a tree?"

"Triples!?" Timmy said or maybe he asked. No one was ever sure.

Timmy wore a Boston Red Sox jersey with a number 8 and the name Yastrzemski printed on the back. Most Milwaukee kids wore Brewers jerseys.

Timmy Kruthers was small and kind of quiet, but when he did speak, it was always different and yet almost always about Milwaukee Brewers players so no one complained.

Timmy never said anything dull or commonplace, but never anything so strange that kids made fun of him either. He added Christmas lights to a regular tree, or something like that, and the amazing thing about him was that he never tried to sound special. He just was.

He did take a lot of crap for being a Red Sox fan and wearing that Red Sox jersey. It was never clear if he actually liked the Red Sox or if he was just a fan of Yastrzemski.

Timmy had seen the Brewers' Sixto Lezcano hit grand slams on two different opening days, the first one in 1978 against Baltimore, and two years later a walk off grand slam against the Red Sox. Anytime a Brewers fan harassed him for wearing a Red Sox jersey, he would recreate the play-by-play of Lezcano's home runs or any great moment in Brewers' history and in doing so, he turned potentially hostile situations into friendly ones, like someone unplugging all the wires from a bomb before the big BOOOOOM!

Timmy knew all the details and Brewers fans appreciated his accuracy, not to mention his unique home run calls. No two were alike, but Frank's favorite was, "Swinging hips, wood meets leather, that ball is on its way to the other side." He threw in all kinds of bizarre details like "ghosts swinging from trees in Perini's Woods."

Lou Perini owned the Boston Braves and moved his team to Milwaukee to begin play at County Stadium in 1953. He installed trees beyond center field and they carried Perini's name until bleachers were added. Old timers who remembered the Braves bought Timmy beers before he reached the legal drinking age.

Timmy loved Milwaukee baseball history, all the way back to the 1890's and over 50 years of American Association minor league Brewers. He wondered how the city seduced the Boston Braves to County Stadium and he glowed over their 13 miracle years before selling out to Atlanta, but "golden minarets never sleep," Timmy would say. "The Seattle Pilots gave birth to the Milwaukee Brewers."

Everyone had a Timmy story. Frank's most memorable was also the most painful. It happened in June of 1984. Frank and Timmy were watching the Brewers on TV, against Boston at Fenway Park. Jim Rice hit two home runs that day, but Timmy had defense on his mind.

"From Ted Williams to Carl Yastrzemski to Jim Rice," Timmy said. "All those left field seasons playing at the school yard because that's what you do at Fenway Park, isn't it? You play. It's a fun house freak show, catching balls off that Green Monster and Carl Yastrzemski…" Timmy didn't finish his sentence. He looked away and smiled.

Frank received a letter from Timmy a few weeks later with a strange sounding city scribbled onto the envelope, somewhere in Oregon. There was also a zip code. Timmy Kruthers was physically gone, something about his dad taking a job in the logging industry.

Frank liked how cities and towns were assigned zip codes. Reminded him of his favorite states on planet earth, those sizzling states like 714 Babe Ruth, .367 Ty Cobb, 511 Cy Young, and his all-time favorite 309 Sam "Wahoo" Crawford because Crawford not only hit 309 career triples, but he also finished with  a career batting average of .309. What were the odds of that!

Klamath Falls, Oregon, zip code 97601, is where Timmy disappeared to. He didn't say much in his initial letter, or anything about baseball anyway, talked mostly about Klamath Falls, about the flora and fauna. Frank had never heard of either word. He looked them up and discovered flora to be plants and fauna animals. That made sense because the second page of Timmy's letter, at the top, said,

*a seagull's cry plays*
*dueling banjos with water*
*lapping over dinosaur back rocks.*

And at the bottom of the same page it said,

*chicken wire cages*
*house the ghosts of eels in a*
*perfume of algae.*

Frank had never seen words arranged like that and had no idea what the hell Timmy was talking about. Maybe it was just a fancy description of birds and plants. Probably, because Timmy closed out the letter with,

*flora and fauna,*
*that's all it ever was and is*
*and always will be.*

Frank showed a fellow fan club member Timmy's letter and he blamed it on California. "Lots of weirdos out there," he said.

Frank said it was Oregon, not California, but another kid said they were the same thing and everyone else agreed and then the original kid who blamed it on California asked, "What kind of kid wears a Carl Yastrzemski Red Sox jersey in Milwaukee anyway?"

And like a chorus in perfect sync, they all said, "A weirdo!"

It was their way of grieving. They missed Timmy, but instead of feeling sentimental, they flushed him down the toilet. It was safer that way, less pain.

Frank remained a devoted Brewers fan and renewed his fan club membership every season. Other than a few pimples on his forehead, life continued to be pretty damn good.

He sat beside his high school locker reading *Baseball Digests* when he should have been setting off fire alarms, disrupting the donut sale, or kissing girls beside the boiler room in the basement.

Frank's favorite Brewer was Ben Oglivie. He loved the way his back arm twitched like Joe Morgan's did and how he was so skinny and still hit so many towering home runs, but most of all, Frank loved the way Oglivie slid into second base. It was the clumsiest thing he had ever seen. It made Oglivie very human.

Frank bought a Ben Oglivie jersey and included a short biography of the Brewers' left fielder in his next letter to Timmy.

> *Hey Timmy:*
>
> *I got your letter and didn't understand too much, but the weather sounds OK out there. I bet you miss baseball. Did you make any new friends? I bought a Ben Oglivie jersey just*

*like your Yastrzemski one, only mine is the Milwaukee Brewers and number 24, not the Red Sox and number 8.*

*Oglivie–Born in Colon, Panama. February 11, 1949. Drafted by the Boston Red Sox in 1968. Traded to the Detroit Tigers in 1973. Traded to the Milwaukee Brewers in 1977 for Jim Slaton and Rich Folkers who never pitched again. The Brewers signed Slaton back the following year. So the Brewers got Oglivie for nothing. Slaton was one of the original Brewers, dating back to 1969. Those weren't even the Brewers. They were the Seattle Pilots. The Brewers weren't an expansion team. Seattle was. Then they relocated to Milwaukee because maybe they went bankrupt. You probably already know all of this. Anyway, that's it for now.*

*P.S. These are tough times. The Brewers haven't been this bad since I started loving them. We almost lost 100 games this year, but it's OK except that Oglivie only hit 12 home runs. He's 35 years old and maybe gonna retire soon?*

*your friend,*
*Frank*

Timmy carried Frank's letter in his jacket pocket for a day or two, read it a few times, and then at a McDonald's restaurant, he sat down and closed his eyes. He took a few deep breaths and focused on Frank, on his greenish blue eyes and then he flipped a McDonald's placemat over and wrote him a letter.

*I'm not far from Chief Seattle, not far from falling off horses. The expansion relocates to Milwaukee and all is lost or all is gained. New perfumes staring at stage coaches and milk delivered in glass bottles, still a few in Ebbets Field moonlight walks and video arcades, pool halls, kissing under grandstands.*

*Dear Frank, I just checked out a book from the library about continental drift, made me think about the Bermuda Triangle, about footprints filled up with water and mud and then drying out and disappearing, but never really disappearing.*

*Maybe one day you'll come and visit and we'll take a trip to Seattle who maybe lost the Pilots, but gained the Mariners.*

*Take care,*
*Timmy*


Frank had never met anyone like Timmy and did everything he could to impress him. It wasn't easy since they were separated by so many rivers and mountains and 2,000 miles and because Timmy seemed so smart and different, but that made it even more intriguing and exciting.

Frank spent hours and sometimes days looking over letters he had already written to Timmy, but never mailed. He wanted them to be the greatest, most interesting things Timmy had ever read and without really knowing it, he started sounding almost as strange as Timmy, using new words and bunching sentences together with less punctuation.

Frank learned about Pangea in English mythology class and then in Earth Science he heard it again. He ran to the post office that same day and sent Timmy the following:

*Dear Timmy,*

> *I thought about you today, probably yesterday too, because when Pangea split, the super-continent let loose a hundred million years cry and rivers of tears sent continents shifting and drifting further apart. Dear sweet gurgle of wild rivers, spawner of salmon, please return home.*

Frank wasn't really sure what he had written, but he sent it to Timmy anyway because it sounded better and more exotic than anything he had ever written.

Timmy's response was the shortest yet and it arrived in less than a week. All it said was,

"*bards of the booth*" and that was followed by Timmy's home run call from a few years earlier, "*Swinging hips, wood meets leather, that ball is on its way to the other side.*"

Frank felt bigger than ever after reading Timmy's letter. He took the home run call as praise for what he had written.

Frank was still a member of the Pepsi Fan Club, but didn't follow the Brewers as closely anymore. Ben Oglivie retired after the 1986 season, and most of the original fan club members had girlfriends or were thinking about college, or jobs, or both.

Frank began to disappear during games, always wandering to the same place, to the concession stand down the left field line. Frank called it his Oracles of Condiment because every time he stood there, beside tubs of ketchup and mustard and between so many Brewers fans, he felt inspired.

The smell of beer was loud and pleasant. It was here where Frank penned his longest letter to Timmy Kruthers. It was more of a confession or a family heirloom.

*Dear Timmy;*

*We didn't laugh about Jimmy Piersall in our house. Half the family was originally from Boston. I don't think I ever told you that Timmy. I guess it didn't matter when we were growing up. Even Grandma knew about Piersall being only 18 when he broke in with the Red Sox. She knew about his antics, suspensions and "tired nerves" and she later understood those nerves to be a severe bipolar struggle. She knew about his time in the Westborough State Hospital.*

*And Grandma knew about Piersall's will and courage and strength and refusal to become stuck on himself. She knew about his comeback, his all-star appearances in 1954 and gold glove in 58. She knew about his playing the shallowest center field in America and still chasing down everything in sight. She knew about his having to replace Dom DiMaggio. She knew and she told us so we all knew—me, my brother Vincent, my two sisters, Mom and Dad, and anyone else who came for dinner.*

*We all fell silent in the house when the words Jimmy Piersall were spoken. He was our Elijah sliding like an apparition through the open*

*door. He was the reminder to let Grandma say*
*what she insisted on telling us,*

*"He (Piersall) made orange juice when the*
*dirty rotten world tossed oranges at him."*

*We didn't have much religion in our house,*
*but we had Jimmy Piersall. We always will.*

*Take care,*
*your friend,*
*Frank*

Timmy received the letter, but could not respond. One month, two months passed, but still no response. Frank kept writing to Timmy, but not about baseball. He wrote about mythology and literature and lyrics to rock and roll songs, about a journey of ancient warriors and their triumph over beasts and impossible odds, about Inns filled with vagabonds and lawyers, judges, priests, and poets, tramps and lovers, plumbers and politicians, all under a big sky.

Still no response.
Frank wrote about the Amazon and its wildlife, shamans and rain forests. He wrote about frozen TV dinners, the first recorded documentary, *Nanook of the North*. He wrote about pinball machines, the art of plumbing in early Indo-Aryan societies, and the history of Milwaukee, especially the great Milwaukee bridge war between Kilbourntown and Juneautown.

Still no response.
He sent Timmy Native American language maps, manifestos, photos and odes to his new favorite Brewer—Rob Deer.

*Hits home runs and strikes out in tornado gushes, walks too but not on defense. He runs and leaps in Knievel bounds and dives and slides across wet grass and is up in a flash throwing missiles to third base.*

Still no response.

A little over one year later, a letter arrived with Klamath Falls on the envelope, but not in Timmy's handwriting. The print was in block letters and very easy to read, the opposite of Timmy's swerves and curves.

Andrew Kruthers informed Frank in a very short and matter of fact letter that his son had suffered a nervous breakdown from exhaustion and nerves and was currently being hospitalized. There was a new address listed for Timmy and an invitation to continue writing him letters. What he didn't tell Frank was that Timmy was being medicated.

Frank didn't consider the timing of his Jimmy Piersall letter synchronizing with Timmy's mental breakdown. Frank felt abandoned and alone more than anything else.

Frank took the Greyhound bus to New York and then California. He hopped trains and slept under bridges, worked as a dishwasher in New York City, and months and years passed and Frank still felt abandoned and alone. He sent Timmy Christmas cards and received cards in return, but Timmy sounded much more serious and kind of dull.

Frank made regular Milwaukee pit stops to visit family, and during one of those visits, he rode the city bus downtown and walked along Lake Michigan. That's where he met Carl Rampage and the two talked for quite some time, mostly about cars. They made plans to meet again.

Carl collected car brochures and attended car shows. He invited Frank to car dealerships around town, and together they test drove Cadillac Fleetwoods and Lincoln Town Cars and visited one dealership after another. Carl was passionate about skyscrapers and airplanes too. He always reminded Frank to "Look up in the sky."

The two of them visited the airport often. They would mix vodka into Sunny Delight orange juice containers and enjoy a *Screwy Delight* while watching planes crawl out to the runway, pick up amazing speed and lift their noses into the sky.

Then they would turn their heads towards a different window and watch planes get bigger and bigger as they lowered to the ground and landed. They developed a knack for doing absolutely nothing and never getting bored. They sat on park benches, loitered in laundromats and hotel lobbies, hung out with panhandlers and learned their nicknames and tales.

Frank felt baseball being reborn inside him. He called it an electromagnetic transfusion and knew that Carl Rampage was responsible, and yet, Frank thought more about Timmy than Carl.

Frank wrote Timmy one letter after another, none more memorable than the one arriving July 7, 2000. Timmy carried it with him for weeks and even gave it a name:

"The Petering Rose."

*Dear Timmy:*

*Well that's a boring way to start a letter. I always loved the way you began with random thoughts. It was like you were welcoming me into your Double Dutch mind if I could follow the flow and crisscross of the strings and then later, in a paragraph or two, you would offer a more formal Dear Frank.*

*I've been thinking about you and hope all is well. Cripes, I don't even know where you live; if you'll even get this letter, but I must do like "Wee Willie" Keeler and keep hitting 'em where they ain't.' I have so much to tell you, probably too much for a letter, but what the hell!*

*Remember that poster of Pete Rose in my bedroom,  the one I ordered from the back of a Wheaties box? I showed it to you that day you came over to my house when we were kids. Anyway, I don't think it cost more than a few proof of purchase seals. It was a simple sketch or not simple because I could never do it. I still have it taped to that same bedroom wall. It looks good beside all the other pennants and pictures. I'm looking at it right now.*

*Rose's profile sits dead center. He has straight brown bangs and that snarl expression on his face, like he's smelling something awful. There's also a second sketch, of a Rose follow through swing. Looks like he's willing a base hit and he probably is. His head scans the ball and I'm sure it goes all twister, mind of its own, eluding a swarm of fielders. He's barely out of the batter's box, but already thinking double.*

*Ty Cobb stands below Rose. His pear-shaped head looks in the opposite direction. The number 4192 is superimposed in yellow score-board lights over Cobb's arm. An oversized bat lays across his left shoulder. But here's the kicker Timmy. For so many years, I only noticed Rose and Cobb. It wasn't all of a sudden, but slowly I started to see more and I think it was around the time I met you.*

*In the foreground of the sketch is a pan-oramic view of Riverfront Stadium. It sits like a donut-shaped spaceship with pillars jetting down from the upper deck like Roman columns. You told me about those columns originating with the Greeks and before that someone else, maybe Egypt? All of it like tree rings rippling backwards through time.*

*To its right is Cincinnati's skyline of three erect buildings. Both the stadium and skyline are pigeon gray and so is the Ohio River and trees along the shore. A small cruise ship can also be seen. The top portion of the poster is volcanic red. It then bleeds into a mellower red where Rose's face begins and fades to yellow and that's where Cobb's ends.*

*All those years I obsessed over baseball and didn't see the Covington Suspension Bridge connecting Ohio and Kentucky and the roll-ing Ohio River as a means of transport and a place for teenagers to explore boundaries and skyscrapers replacing churches in man's attempt to reach heaven, the stadium architecture, building materials, human toil and strain, the heave and ho.*

*I just wanted baseball to go on forever and ever but then as I got older, it felt so stupid to feel that way, but not now. I feel the same way about baseball all over again. I'm not so ashamed anymore and good thing too because baseball doesn't hold grudges. It welcomed me back like wide open Catholic Church doors. There looked to be even more to discover this time around.*

*By the way, the Brewers drafted Ben Sheets with the 10th pick in this year's draft. Here's to hopefully a future ace.*

*Your friend,*
*Frank*

It was like a weight lifted from Frank's shoulders. He stood up straight like a tree and felt free to explore like never before. There were candy stores to revive his old habit of buying wax packs of baseball cards. There was also Gonzaga Hall.

The cramped room of Gonzaga was inside the St. Alyosius Church on Milwaukee's west side. It housed baseball card dealers from all over the Midwest every two months. There was no room to walk. That's where Frank learned about middle-aged men with wild, greasy hair and body odor and booze-flavored breath before noon.

Frank spent 50 dollars on a 1960 Topps Carl Yastrzemski rookie card, and on the bus ride home wrote Timmy a letter, but it was Sunday. The post office was closed. Frank could have slapped a stamp on the envelope and stuffed It in a mailbox, but he loved the post office. It was his little *Socotra Islands*, Egyptian Pyramids, Cooperstown, New York and anonymous day trip along the dirty local river all rolled into one.

So Timmy waited until morning and took the bus downtown. He walked towards the Juneau Street Post Office and it felt like 10,000 dust particles were being set free. Frank moved in gallops and once inside, he rejected the world machine stamp, $1.78 postage paid sticker. He insisted on sorting through individual stamps.

There were dragon flies, ladybugs, a giant octopus, and caterpillars. He licked and pasted them to his letter and walked to the drop off box. That's when he spotted the display case-*Baseball's Legendary Playing Fields*. There were 20 stamps in all. Frank scanned from left to right—Crosley Field, Fenway Park, Polo Grounds, Tiger Stadium, Old Comis.....

"Psssst."

A man wearing a long beige trench coat and a baseball hat paced back and forth in front of the display case.

"Psssst, Frank."

Frank didn't look up, but then it happened again,

"Pssssst, Frank," followed by "Frank, come here."

There was no Yastrzemski jersey, but it was definitely Timmy Kruthers. He hadn't grown an inch, just a bigger belly and the beginnings of a beard. Frank never imagined this moment, never practiced or rehearsed for it.

"How did you know I would be here?" Frank asked in a shy whisper.

Timmy didn't bother answering. He lunged towards Frank and they embraced. There was only one thing to do. Take Timmy Kruthers to the Chinese restaurant across the street where Tsingtao beer taps were one dollar.

"Here's to passenger pigeons, Ellis Valentine, long distance communication, and your return to Milwaukee," Frank said, still shaking with excitement.

They clanked glasses and drank their beer.

"I haven't seen you in 10 years," Frank continued, "But here we are behaving like an extra innings game."

"Maybe I'll be happier here than in Oregon, said Timmy, "I didn't tell anyone I was leaving, not even my dad."

"Better to be at a bar, drinking beer with a buddy, and Brewers baseball right around the corner, don't you think Timmy?"

"Well, I was really bored out there," admitted Timmy. "Maybe you're right. I was bored without baseball."

Frank began to bang on the rail and sing, "Milwaukeee, Menomineeee, Kinnickinnic" and then he did it again and one more time.

"Beer in the late afternoon will do that to you," said Timmy. "I'll buy the next round." Timmy flagged down the bartender and ordered two shots and two more beers. Frank slid off the bar stool and simulated a gymnast dismounting from the crossbar. Timmy clapped. They crashed glasses again, drank some more, ordered a pizza, drank a little more and Frank wasn't nervous anymore.

He reached into his backpack and removed a notebook, fingered through a few pages and found something. He handed it to Timmy.

**_and the animals didn't seem to mind_**

_the martians that made robots_
_that made the yankees hate the red sox_
_prudes the pornos_

*pornos the prudes*
*muslims the jews*
*jews the muslims*
*betty crockers the frankensteins*
*1's the 0's*
*snatched up the sandwich board war.*
*A deer felt the scene was safe enough*
*to leg up from the milwaukee river*
*cross the north avenue bridge*
*and lap up a beer at the rail with a pack of drunk humans.*
*It was 5:30 am in the future.*

Frank didn't let Timmy respond. He grabbed his shoulders and lifted him off the barstool and onto the floor, refusing to let go. The two spun around while Timmy repeated the lines about "the Yankees hating the Red Sox." They laughed and spun around some more, pausing long enough to enjoy drinks compliments of the bartender. The night then slipped into a comfortable blur.

Frank poked Timmy with a long stick. The two had wandered south after the drinking, dancing and pizza and passed out in the small park behind the Milwaukee Historical Society. Timmy rocked into the lotus position and before opening his eyes, the previous night came back to him like a slide show.

"Shakespeare and The Beer Barrel Polka," laughed Timmy.

They walked to McDonald's. Timmy stood in line and ordered coffees. Frank disappeared to the pay phone, called Carl, and invited him for breakfast. He lived around the corner. Frank watched Carl pull into the McDonald's parking lot in a white car.

"Here comes my friend Carl. I want you to meet him Timmy."

"Is that a Lincoln Town car?" asked Timmy.

"Lincoln shmincoln," said Frank. "It's just a name."

"Just a name, said Timmy, "Like Chet Lemon was just a name?"

"Yes, but Chet Lemon was not a lemon," said Frank. "He was an outfielder."

"And Reggie Cleveland was not from Cleveland," said Timmy.

"That's right," said Frank. "He was born in Swift Current, Saskatchewan."

"And Daryl Boston was born in Cincinnati," added Timmy.

Carl had already entered McDonald's and sat down next to Frank. He caught the tail end of the name game and shook his head. "Don't tell me your friend is a baseball freak too?" asked Carl with a half-smile.

"But Pete Rose did have a tint of rose in his cheeks," said Frank, ignoring Carl for the moment.

"And Rusty Staub's auburn colored hair looked rusty in the right light," said Timmy.

"But Dick Green was definitely not green," screamed Frank.

"And Vida Blue was not blue and Red Schoendienst not red," said Timmy in a much softer voice.

"This is an Early Wynn for us," Frank said and he was right. McDonald's was still serving breakfast and so Frank asked Carl if he would like a green tea, but before he could answer, Timmy said, "That would definitely be an Herb Score."

All three of them laughed.

"You know I don't care too much about baseball," Carl said, "But I have my Dad's Lincoln Town Car today and there is a Brewers game going on, isn't there? I can drive."

It was the middle of April. The Astros were in town. The three of them arrived to Miller Park in time to see the brand new retractable roof open. It was a huge deal to Carl who grunted like someone watching a peep show for the first time. Timmy watched Carl watching the roof open for the entire 10 minutes. It was hard to tell who was more mesmerized.

Frank reached into his backpack, removed a notebook, and began to write:

*things I learned at a baseball game*
*looking back now*
*i was like Buddha when*
*he first witnessed old age, dying, and all that*
*deflecting my mind outside the cushioned shoe box castle*
*to a lonely road.*

*i was hand in hand with my dad*
*walking through county stadium parking tunnels,*
*a tailgater paradise, a tailgater whiskey gone violent.*
*i learned one push lays a dude down.*

*two fisted slopper downing backwash*
*talking to imaginary gods on the pay phone.*
*i learned integrity wears wet eyes.*

*couples grooving under the bleachers,*
*i learned Cecil Cooper home runs and making out*
*offer the same excitement.*

*and inside the stadium,*
*urinal troughs.*
*i learned all piss exits the same drain.*

*

There was a home run hit in the second inning, but not by the Brewers. It was the Astros' Lance Berkman and the Milwaukee crowd became quiet. Timmy asked Carl about his family. Frank opened his notebook a second time and began to write:

### the lick of hysteria

*i'm a sucker for the home run.*
*it's the sin of expectation lust*
*and Bernie's beer-barreled chalet is king.*

*we all know enough science*
*so when the batter lacking atlas*
*swags to home plate,*
*we fans understand*
*wind and combustion.*

*we know hips hands and luck can suddenly sync*
*and when that spheroid spins from the pitcher's tarantula grip*
*and 60 feet 6 inches later*
*a perfect jericho sounds*
*and the ball sails....*
*we are the ball*
*rising up and out of body and mind,*
*a momentary release,*
*dancing with strangers in tailgate parking lots*
*long after the last out.*

*

The Brewers trailed the Astros 7-1 heading into the bottom of the ninth. Carl reached under his seat and pretended to be tying his shoes while mixing cocktails from the orange juice and vodka he had smuggled into the game.

Frank opened his notebook for a third time and began to write:

### 309 is where I really wanna be
*It's more than Sam Wahoo Crawford.*
*it's space sucked from stadium outfield alleys*
*and it reeks of "speed up the god damn game,"*
*but a triple is still a tornado*
*and fielders still transform from stuffed diplomats*
*into stumbling drunks*
*as the ball bursts like gutter water*
*caroming in a bad dream chase*
*the hero and his net slipping*
*while the batter is all wild west*
*gunning round the bandit paths in full abandon*
*his helmet no longer needed*
*and we fans riot*
*because unlike a home run*
*the ball is still in play.*

# Thunderheart and the New Addictions

On sunny days, prisms of light made their way inside. On cloudy days, a duller glare ricocheted off Sunkist Astros emblems and turned the room into marmalade. The 92nd Street Orphanage housed 40 boys and girls born from mothers addicted to moonshine, gambling, sex—40 different horror stories dumped at the doorsteps of The Moderation Room in Bolduck, Wisconsin.

The town's name may have sounded plentiful, but free will in Bolduck was nothing more than choosing a match, bic, or zippo to set oneself on fire.

Jeffrey Thunderheart was no different. He was raised by an addicted mother and dropped at the doorsteps of The Moderation Room with a bike, a bag, and his whole life in front of him. But Thunderheart saw endless circles where the other 39 forgotten ones saw squares and ends.

Thunderheart's birth certificate said Galveston, Texas, but he had never been there, only knew it was raided by Spanish Pirates who called it the "Island of Doom." No one at 92nd Street had ever been to Texas. Jeffrey Thunderheart was too young to know why, but that was about to change.

He squeezed Tabasco eye drops onto peoples' plates, and if that didn't get his fellow Orphies (Orphans for Life) roused, he skunked their ass in ping-pong, checkers, or Go Fish. Anything to crack their minds and slip 'em an idea in their most vulnerable state, sway their focus onto Colt Stadium—the new home of the Houston Colt .45s baseball team.

Thunderheart identified nine potentials in the winter of 1963—one year after major league baseball welcomed Houston into its exclusive National League. Thunderheart knew damn well the chosen ten would never reach Texas, not in 1963 anyway. The windows were reinforced with steel bars and the barbed wire fence surrounding the compound was electric, but those were nothing but symbols and a colt .45 was the single action revolver "that won the west."

There were rumors of rattle snakes at Colt Stadium and a mosquito population of biblical proportions, but Thunderheart paid no attention to news and naysaying. He kept the course, determined to reach Houston one day.

The kids ran away, but only until their stomachs growled and they raced back home to the orphanage for meat and ice cream scoops of potatoes. They were barely teenagers, but Thunderheart made damn sure they were all hooked on Spaghetti Westerns—the gateway drug to stampedes, cowboy hats, and ultimately, Colt .45s baseball.

Life settled into a routine like anywhere else, up at dawn for morning exercises, off to school and back home for dinner and sleep at the Orphanage. Cold Wisconsin winters gave way to lush, humid summers, round and round with very few disruptions, but a change in Houston meant a change at 92nd Street.

So when the Colt .45s became the Astros and the Wild West was swallowed up by the Astrodome, Thunderheart requested the windows of the Moderation Room be opened during the day. He used air as an argument, to respect what Astros players now lacked.

Orphan Mommy and Daddy soon softened their cold-hearted stance. Garlic breaths gave way to spring blossom. The windows were opened. A Walt Disney-like feeling spread across the Moderation Room. A glaze could be seen in the head-master's eyes—a Salt Lake City salvation glaze. Thunderheart could feel the loosening. He seized the opportunity and turned arts and crafts hour into a lock and load ammunition session. Orphies clipped Sunkist orange Astros colors from construction paper and presented the shapes as gifts to surrogate Mommy and Daddy who bit the bait.

The Orphies gathered at the scrabble table and watched with amusement as their bosses fell mesmerized by the orange distraction. Thunderheart sang songs about the big red baron—Rusty Staub, and Little Joe Morgan. He smuggled baseball cards and a short wave radio into the grounds.

The boys skipped morning calisthenics, choosing to imitate Morgan's batting stance twitch instead. A network of wires soon crisscrossed the room at twilight, invisible to the night guards, but from a small speaker came the play-by-play voice of Gene Elston for all Orphies to hear. Breakfast was not eaten, showers not needed. There were box scores to scan.

Then Joe Morgan and Cesar Geronimo were dealt to the Reds and the Orphie's fever vanished. They became law-abiding young men. Only Thunderheart carried on in secret, sounding out the names Roger Metzger and César Cedeño, the extra vowels serving as his own retaliatory Astros mantra. But it wasn't enough.

Good behavior prevailed. Astros fever was nowhere to be found. The Orphies were awarded an experimental release. Thunderheart endured a secret investigation, but he too was set free.

Local families served as hosts. Mothers prepared hot meals and fathers dug out mitts from long ago places for a game of mythic catch with their stand-in sons. There was soon talk of adoption, but when a revolution happened in Houston, one also happened to the Orphies.

Naval architect and marine engineer Dr. John McMullen bought the Astros as well as Texas's native son, Nolan Ryan. Joe Morgan returned. The Astros started winning and the liberated residents of The 92nd Street Orphanage drank and smoked and sniffed in celebration, and each and every one of them was admitted not back to the The Orphanage, but to Bolduck's lone drug and alcohol rehabilitation center.

Thunderheart was one of the first to be locked down. He arrived after a two-week stay in Bolduck General Hospital, recovering from cough syrup poisoning. He led chants of Jose Cruuuuuuuz and Terry Puuuuuuhl as his old Orphie pals were escorted one by one into the rehab center. They were reunited, and orange filled the air again. Thunderheart referred to everyone as Habbers, short for rehabilitators for life.

The Orphies became Habbers in 1979, the same year James Rodney (J.R.) Richard struck out 313 batters, and when Richard suffered a stroke the following year, the Habbers began to shake and speak in tongues. A few dug out Pentecostal scrapbooks, inserting James and Rodney where Solomon and Enoch were supposed to be sung. The rehab facility was forced into lock down mode as federal troops were called in to investigate the "suspicious, religious-like fervor."

Richards pitched his last game of the 1980 season on July 14th, but that didn't stop the Habbers. They kept on singing and chanting J.R.'s name and the Astros kept on winning, right up until the last game of the season—a do or die shootout against the second place Dodgers, who had won three in a row against the Astros, leaving both teams with identical 91-70 records.

But Joe Niekro put an end to any miracle Dodgers finish by knuckling the Astros to a complete game win—his 20th of the season, sending Houston to the post season for the first time in franchise history. And in the playoffs, the Astros were leading the Phillies 5-2 in the decisive game five of the N.L. Championship with prodigal Texas son Nolan Ryan on the Astrodome mound. Just nine more outs till the World Series when Philadelphia shockingly drove Ryan to the showers, scoring five times to take a 7-5 lead.

Habbers flipped wood chairs upside down and banged away on makeshift bongos, and what do you know, the Astros rallied to tie the score in the bottom of the 8th on a Jose Cruz single. But when Gary Maddox doubled in the 10th and Houston failed to score in the bottom half, Habbers grabbed those same bongo chairs and swung them wildly at the overhead lights. The room grew darker with every smashed bulb. The damage had been done. Additional guards were called in to maintain peace and order.

Thunderheart encouraged people in power to sit Habbers down and force them to watch a replay of Game 5 on a regular basis.

"It will make your job much easier," Thunderheart promised. "Seeing Ryan surrender a three-run lead like that will sedate Habbers into a comatose state, and if that doesn't do the trick, the 10th inning will."

And Thunderheart was absolutely right. Habber faces drooped and they began to move like zombies, barely lifting their feet when they walked. Authorities were once again convinced that all traces of Astros passion had been extinguished. They loosened their grip and let Habbers be. Thunderheart celebrated quietly for he had dodged a Colt .45 bullet. The vision was still intact.

He knew induced tranquility to be the calm side of the double helix inside Habbers' addictive minds. It was a two-headed monster, and when baseball suffered a strike the following season, Thunderheart sensed a spark. He blamed baseball authorities, arousing the other side of his fellow Habbers. The vision of one day reaching Texas now had an added incentive: to defy all worldly authorities.

Thunderheart received his first issue of Astros Times by mail in the winter of 1982. He requested the five-page newsletter be stuffed in a plain white envelope with "no Astros traces anywhere" and so when an issue arrived, no one suspected a thing.

The back page featured a harmless, but heartwarming story about Astros players, none more hair-raising than the winter issue of 1984. It was barely a paragraph long and all it really said was something about Mike Scott having a rendezvous in Detroit, but to Thunderheart, it was a powder keg.

He mickeyed Habber heads with a tall tale about a secret meeting between pitcher Mike Scott and a mysterious Mr. Roger Craig, pitching coach supreme of the World Champion Tigers, and then Thunderheart added in a whisper, "to pass on the esoteric technique needed to throw a split-fingered fastball. It's a thing of beauty, the way it drops like a melted ice cream cone."

The Habbers were sucked in and watched with amazement as the 1985 season launched and Scott started getting batters out and winning games galore—18 in all. And the following year they fell out of their skin when Scott almost topped J. R. Richard as the Astro's single season strikeout king.

"Who strikes out 306 batters as a 31-years old?" Thunderheart asked triumphantly. "Scott's older than all of us." Habbers began speaking statistical whispers in the corridor. "Pitching, pitching, and more pitching—the only way to win in the Astrodome."

They learned how to hold a split-fingered fastball, or tried to anyway, and in the process turned the lunch room into a rifle range with potatoes, oranges, and apples flying all about with no day more rocking than September 25, 1986. "Pandemonium" is what the Bolduck Times headline called it and rightly so. Mike Scott had pitched a no-hitter that afternoon. A notable event for sure, but nothing new. It was the 8th no-hitter in Astros history and not too newsworthy in Bolduck, Wisconsin, but what pushed Habbers over the edge was that the Astros also clinched the National League West that day.

Habbers set fire to orange sunkist decorations and danced wild as the walls burned. The police and fire departments rushed to the scene, but not before errant split-fingered potato tosses shattered windows, and one by one the Habbers escaped into the late afternoon. A few hopped southbound trains towards larger Wisconsin cities. Others followed the river and hid in the woods on the outskirts of town.

Rehab reps and local police concluded that the young men were not schooled in the ways of surviving the wild, that it was only a matter of time before they surfaced in society, looking for food and water. And the Habbers did come out of hiding, but for very different reasons.

They had each found a way to watch Game 6 of the 1986 National League Playoffs. Some slipped into bars and observed quietly from the rail. Others listened from the woods, under the stars, on radios they had brought with them.

And when the Astros lost the 16-inning marathon to the New York Mets and were once again eliminated from the play-offs, just like 1980, the defeat was too much to digest, even for Thunderheart. He wandered city streets where pills were as plentiful as green bibles, and whatever junkies offered, whether it be Morphine, Valium, or Codeine, Thunderheart popped it. He eventually made his way to the Last Straw Saloon and his magic tongue took care of the rest. Strangers bought him drinks, and one too many Whiskeys later, he must have passed out because next thing he knew he was back at the Rehab Center.

Thunderheart waited patiently for the other nine Habbers to be caught and returned, and when they were, he waited some more as they recovered from their respective overdoses. And when the moment was right and everyone had enough coffee swimming in their blood stream, he raised his clenched fist and declared that, "This was only the beginning. There will be more next year."

The Rehab Center was one of my daily medical supply delivery runs and typically required a dolly and some heavy lifting. I'll never forget the day there was only one box. The sun was shining so I parked a few blocks away and walked. Violet bulbs on branches had already exploded into green leafy spiders. It was spring regardless of what the calendar said.

The place looked more like a castle from the outside. The bricks were limestone and the two connecting buildings formed a triangle shape and featured a rusty minaret on top. The corridor was cold with a tall spacious ceiling like the inside of a subway or Cathedral. I was wearing gym shoes with rubber soles, but the echo was cowboy boot big.

A young man with a full head of curly hair greeted me at the door. I had never seen him before. A nurse typically signed for packages and then directed me where to complete the delivery. I recognized a few employees in the background and they showed no signs of resistance so I let this guy sign for the package and lead me down the corridor.

As the gate closed behind us, he began gushing about the Astros, from Rusty Staub to Enos Cabell and Bill Doran, who he insisted was the team's most valuable player last year. I thought it was a bit strange to talk about the Astros in Bolduck, Wisconsin, but it was my last delivery of the day and I was ahead of schedule. I had time to waste so I set the box down in the corner of the utility closet and listened.

The guy walked towards the window and began to whisper. It was his way of defying the nurses I guess. They looked on with mild curiosity. I imagined them shaking their heads and rolling their eyes like a wife might do to her husband after 20 years of marriage. He extended his hand and introduced himself as Jeffrey Thunderheart.

"So what if Jose Cruz is 38. He still hit .300 last year. I don't think he's going to retire. Do you think he's going to retire?" Thunderheart didn't look very long at me, but his eyes were still. It was like he could see right through me with one quick glance.

"Mike Scott and… well, yes, we can include Nolan Ryan," he continued. "Both of them in the same starting staff…" and then he grabbed me by the elbow and said, "Glen Davis hit 31 home runs last year and I think 20 of 'em were in the Dome."

I tried to slip in some sober reality about the problem being the rest of the offense not scoring enough runs and that a slump here or there by one of them or even worse, a season ending injury and the whole offense could tank, but Thunderheart lived up to his name.

"We got nothing to lose. We're gonna keep the rally alive no matter what it takes. Every one of us a player-manager in full control of our lives. We'll see the nurses as the ones behind the aquarium glass. We're going to Houston this year."

"If you give me your mailing address," I said, "We can stay in touch during the seas…" Thunderheart didn't let me finish my sentence. He had bigger plans for us and wouldn't take no for an answer. He walked me to the other side of the room, looked out the window facing east, and asked,

"Where is it?"

"Where's what?" I asked.

"You know, the getaway car. You came here in a van, right?"

I knew what he was thinking and it felt so crazy I had to do it, but I couldn't.

"Meet us right there." Thunderheart pointed to a small alley between a dry cleaner and a 7/11. "Turn the lights off on the van and wait. It may take us a while to complete our escape, but we'll be there Saturday night, after sundown and so will you, right?"

I smiled at first and laughed along, tried to be diplomatic. Thunderheart didn't buy it. He knew there was something else inside me, something buried but still alive. I put my arm on his shoulder and told him I wasn't that crazy. I couldn't steal the van from work and lose my job. I had bills to pay.

He wouldn't take no for an answer and led me to the door. He bowed and shot me a glance I still can't get out of my head. His eyes rolled up and into the back of his head. Only two white ovals remained.

I'm not a religious person, but something happened at work that brought me to my knees. I returned to the warehouse and sat down in the back room with Terri, my second-generation Sicilian boss, and Carlos his assistant. I noticed the clock on the wall wasn't working.

Terri accused Carlos of stealing supplies and reselling them on the black market. Carlos confessed with sarcasm.

"Yeh, I like hanging around old age homes and dealing Depends Diapers to the elderly," Carlos laughed. "That's why I drive a Trans-Am with tinted windows you stupid Sicilian bastard!"

Terri jumped up from his swivel chair and drove it into Carlos who fell immediately to the floor. They rolled around a while. Punches were thrown. The fight spilled onto the street. The cops showed up, and as Terri was stuffed into the back seat of a squad car, he instructed me to lock up the store.

"Keep the van until I get back" were his parting words. It was all too perfect. Jeffrey Thunderheart and Houston were too tempting to resist and now I had a van.

I waited more than an hour Saturday night, but Thunderheart and nine others eventually raced across the street. I watched them in the rear view mirror. They were moving fast, and once inside the med supplies van, they were like kids set free on a playground, crawling every which way, and why wouldn't they after all those years cooped up inside institutions! This would probably be the first road trip of their lives.

I had a job and the outward appearance of being organized. I paid my rent and took out my trash on Tuesdays. My life followed a very predictable routine. I was excited too.

We made one stop—the Salvation Army to pick up floor mats so the Habbers could sleep if they decided to. We had 1200 miles and 36 hours to reach Houston in time for Opening Day. We merged onto highway 55 south, just outside of Chicago. That's where Kevin Bass entered the conversation. I knew Bass as the prospect Milwaukee traded for Don Sutton in 1982. The Habbers knew him as a .311 hitter who hit 20 home runs the previous year, "but didn't walk very much," someone whispered from the back of the van, and with that, everyone yelled in unison,

"Griiiiiiiiinch."

Thunderheart waved his hands, an indication for everyone to quiet down, and everyone did. It was impressive the way they followed his lead like an orchestra does their conductor.

"Let's stop and buy poles and worms," Thunderheart insisted. "We'll fish along the Illiniois River and catch our own bass."

No one said anything so I assumed all were on board with Thunderheart's plan to go fishing, but then that same voice shot up from the back of the van. It sounded more like a high-pitched whistle. It was Vincent, and this surprised everyone, including Thunderheart, because Vincent was the quietest of the Habbers, or at least he was when living under the Rehab center's rules. But he was free now and enjoying the wind. His tongue loosened.

"Mike Scott is scheduled to face Orel Hershiser in less than 24 hours," Vincent said. There was a pause for a good 20 seconds and then he added in a loud, robotic monotone voice, "And we're going to be there."

"Scott came so damn close to winning 20 games last year," said Thunderheart. "A few more runs here or there and that would have been something. Only been two 20-game winners in Astros history."

"Four," corrected Vincent, "Or actually only three since Niekro did it twice." Vincent snapped his finger so the the guy sitting next to him could hear. He had his head buried in a baseball records book and now he looked up at Vincent, nodded, and dove back into the book, rifling through pages in search of what I assumed was info on Astros' 20-game winners. He eventually came up for air and announced that,

"Larry Dierker won 20 games in 1969. J.R. Richard did the same in 1976."

The sound of Richard's name sent everyone into a frenzy, stomping their feet and cheering in unison, *J-A-M-E-S R-O-D-N-E-Y R-I-C-H-A-R-D* with some extra ooomph added to the *C-H-A-R-D*, turned the pitcher's name into a song. The guy with the records book tried to read on, "Joe Niekro won 21 games in 1979 and followed it up with 20 in 1980," but the Habbers were still singing about J.R. and didn't hear a damn thing.

Quiet overtook the van as we crossed into Texas. We rode along in silent anticipation until signs for the Astrodome began to appear as mile markers—50...25...10. Thunderheart then suggested we grill some sausages, and his idea quickly grew into a crusade.

My mind drifted back to the County Stadium parking lot where I used to walk around, watching others enjoy the pre-game ritual of tailgating. I started wondering again if maybe I missed out on something significant, something bigger than myself, the peace that comes from being part of a community. Maybe the brats, beer, open air and camaraderie had become even more important now that friends were harder to come by and death was no longer impossible.

"We need to eat," Thunderheart insisted, "And when was the last time we enjoyed a big barbecue? Have we ever?"

We shot up highway 45 to the Walmart Supercenter and picked up a mini grill, a bag of charcoal, lighter fluid, and then raced across the street for some beer, burgers, brats, hot dogs, buns and chips. We followed the Old Spanish Trail and slipped into a parking lot on the corner of Fannin and Holly Hall Streets and received some strange looks from Astros fans. Thunderheart wasn't the least bit shy. I think he felt right at home among all those cowboy hats. He ripped open the bag of charcoal and arranged them on the grill floor with incredible accuracy, like he'd tailgated a dozen times before, though in fact he was very much a virgin.

About a dozen Astros fans gathered round and Thunderheart discussed the various meats he was preparing and wondered out loud just how good Dickie Thon might have been. The locals took an immediate liking to Thunderheart.

They knew about County Stadium tailgating and welcomed the idea to Houston, especially since the Brewers were far away in that other league with the designated hitter. We talked and ate and good thing someone mentioned the Wild West cartoon shootouts on the Astrolite scoreboard. It reminded us that we still didn't have tickets to the game, so we made our way towards the Astrodome, to hopefully scalp left field lower box seats, to join in chants of Cruuuuuuuuuuuuuuz.

Unfortunately, we never even made it across the street.

A man with a handlebar mustache stood in our way. He wanted a hamburger and had never seen a "parking lot cook up" as he called it. Vincent took an immediate liking to the man. Vincent was tall and skinny, wore glasses, and everyone seemed to trust his instincts, because they all turned around and returned to the van.

"It's tailgating," Vincent explained, his eyes wide open now and his mild hunchback slowly straightening out. He looked happy. "The grill was a $19.99 Walmart special, no more than 2 inches off the ground," Vincent continued. "Looks like a dome." The man with a handlebar mustache moved closer to Vincent.

We had already grilled the brats, but there were a few more hamburger patties and plenty of chips and beer. I began to wonder about this guy asking for a burger. Had he been watching us? Did he follow us to Walmart? I was the only one wondering.

"You guys got it all wrong," said the man." I could feel the air being sucked out of our sails. Suddenly, the mission was in jeopardy. The urgency to get into the game and see batting practice was slipping away, replaced by a new obsession—this strange-looking man speaking with an Italian accent.

"The delicacy of wild roasted pinashin," he said, "is believed to be a cousin of the South American rabbit. It's so rare that no taxonomy is available. But I've tasted the meat and I can tell you it's ideal for this tailgating séance you so obviously enjoy." The man put his hand on Vincent's shoulder and continued.

"You see, the sizzle and open air, not to mention camaraderie all around is perfect for the pinashin, relaxes the flesh so
it cooks slow and all the way through. The crunch and juice
and flavor are impossible to describe. The sizzle sound changes
when it's ready to be devoured. We're talking no more than
seven minutes, tailor-made for the tailgate, no?"

I sort of anticipated what would come next and I began to
worry not so much about batting practice, but Mike Scott's first
pitch. The strange man pulled out a map of some obscure town
on the northern tip of Uruguay where it was believed the last
of the pinashin were seen.

I was the one with a van and immediately told them no
way, but the strange man stopped me mid-sentence and saved
me from looking unreasonable in the eyes of the Habbers, who
had now entered a binge phase. He offered to drive them, first
to Las Mochis, Mexico and from there, a series of trains, ships
and roads to a town in Uruguay that no one but Vincent could
pronounce.

And that's exactly how it ended. Jeffrey Thunderheart and
the nine Habbers walked away. They were like a dream to me,
here and gone in a 26 hour, 1200 mile flash, onto something
new or maybe not. I didn't know if the strange man had followed us from Bolduck, Wisconsin. Maybe he was hired to
retrieve the Habbers and return them to the Rehab Center.

I could have followed them to find out, but I was in Houston,
Texas and it was opening day. I was alone, and scalping a ticket
would be a cinch. So that's exactly what I did. My seat was
nowhere near left field, but Jose Cruuuuuuuz hit a two-out
home run in the bottom of the 7th inning, gave the Astros a 4-3
lead, and made a winner out of Mike Scott.

I exited the Astrodome and zigzagged across the parking lot, feeling euphoric. There were five games remaining on the homestand and mats in the back of the van. Astros junkie. I liked the sound of it.

# Make Me One with Everything

An old man encouraged me to develop weak ideas and inferior love. He guaranteed that if I present this concept to my subconscious a miracle would happen. I would be able to love more than one significant other.

He was well aware that I might hate him at first. After all, it would be a major blow to the *happily ever after* relationship crutch I had concocted in my mind, but he believed in me. And so he waited for that inevitable day when I would crawl back to his mythical dugout and crown him my manager.

It's hard to pinpoint the exact moment I realized the world was held together by thirty baseball fanatics, but I'm pretty sure it happened after I let the old man's promise marinate a while inside me. I must have sensed the significance because I ran downstairs in the opposite direction of my baseball card collection.

I felt naked and vulnerable, but didn't drown the darkness with colorful 1975 Topps baseball cards like I had so many times before. I went elsewhere, to a spot under the basement steps where my brother typically smooched with his girlfriend(s). Initials were carved on the wall in the shape of hearts. More than one. It was there beside the ghost of kisses past that it dawned on me. These 30 baseball fanatics set the world on fire and kept it aglow 365 days a year.

I still didn't know what my role would be in all of this. You can imagine how nervous I was. It would be like getting a phone call from Jesus himself saying, "Hey, it's me. Just wanted to let you know it's all true. And you're a part of it." That's why I escaped to the basement. It was like summer suddenly arriving and being forced to strip down to shorts and a T-shirt after five long months hiding behind animal furs.

That old man also warned me to keep my distance from fanatics because they lived real close to the source. I assumed he was referring to the center of the earth where there's molten lava and what not, hot as hell. He didn't tell me to avoid them, but to just try and ease my way in because getting too close too fast would be like getting too close to a fire. "If you're not careful," he said, "You'll get burned." I looked down at my feet and wiggled my toes. I was wearing two pairs of socks and black shoes, but I could feel them. This was all really happening.

I eventually crawled out from under the basement steps and into the light of my father's tool room, never straying too far. As a matter of fact, I never left the basement once I realized the earth was hanging on the whims of these 30 anonymous baseball fanatics. I needed some time to fill out a lineup card and consider my next move. This was going to be a big game, maybe the biggest game of my life.

I started to memorize everything ever written about baseball and I soon experienced what religious people call an epiphany. I dragged all my baseball card doubles down stairs and lined them up in protective stacks. I created a home run wall, a fortress, with 1979 Topps baseball cards. There was no shortage of material. I remember that baseball card hunting season real well. I had labored until early August before finally finding my coveted Gorman Thomas card to complete the set. By that time, I had amassed more than 4,000 doubles including nine Ed Ott's.

Just beyond my fortification, we had a small annex of a room where my father stashed his old wooden skis and spare tires. Our family called it the "tire room" and exiled people there when they misbehaved. No one took me seriously when I packed up the rest of my cards – mostly rookie stars from the late 80's, a few tattered cards from the 1960's, my baseball books, and Strat-O-Matic paraphernalia and transformed that tiny bomb shelter of a tire room into Cooperstown's west wing. It wasn't too long before they started calling me "Knucklehead."

It dawned on me as I rifled through Rookie of the Year lists that maybe my obsession with names and numbers was somehow connected with the overabundance of names present in the Old Testament. If you believe the book came from God, then you probably hold every word to be true. According to this reasoning, the deepest proverb was only as true as the name Enosh, as in Enos Slaughter. That was some kind of name, both his first and last. Enosh from the bible lived to be 905 years old. Believe it or not, that was normal back then. I guess the air was cleaner.

And Slaughter? Well, it doesn't get any more gruesome than killing so many people at one time, and Enos Slaughter—the Hall of Fame outfielder passed away in 1986. As in "86ed." But more importantly, the number in reverse is 68, as in 1968. That's the number that really blew my mind because Denny McLain registered a WHIP (hits + walks divided by innings pitched) of .905 in the year, you guessed it—1968—and that

WHIP is identical to Enosh's lifespan of 905 years. It's best to stop my polymania before it reaches the manic stage.

What's more important is that I was beginning to better understand my role. These thirty baseball fanatics were trying to communicate with me. I opened a Ring Lardner anthology with renewed vigor and then suddenly set it down. Questions filled my mind. Was Tommy Agee's last name the shortest ever by a Rookie of the Year winner? Or was it Mel Ott? Ron Cey? Carlos Lee? A Japanese player I never knew named Ko?

Days turned into nights and winter became spring. I found myself sleeping besides unread stacks of magazines. Mom left books about baseball's first teams, like the Braves, Pirates, and Red Sox, outside the tire room door when she delivered lunch or dinner. These were wonderful tomes written with words like *swashbuckled*, *flabbergasted*, and *juggernaut*.

There was a world outside the green cement blocks encasing me. I heard bits and pieces in between innings of Bob Uecker's radio play by play, all the commercial interruptions, like when a neighbor spots a Mr. Johnson barbecuing brats and announces it over a loudspeaker. Next thing you know, Mr. Johnson is entertaining friends he never knew he had. This was only an ad on the radio for Johnsonville Brats, but I took it as a definite sign of life.

I scanned the long list of players who had passed away–the dead zone–and I did it to ready myself for the opposite, for life. It was a very comprehensive list with detailed accounts of what pulled them under. My favorite was John Ake who drowned trying to row across the Mississippi. I had no choice but to become a Samurai warrior. I feared nothing. Good thing, too, because smoke plumes set sail from the Pittsburgh Pirates ashtray. They swirled and curved and darted and took on very human shapes. The ashtray was made of black glass. The inscription was the box score from Game 7 of the 1960 World Series in gold writing. It immediately clicked that these smoky shapes were watching me. Imagine my anxiety! I had just finished reading about Mr. Ake drowning when abracadabra, these little ghosts started rising from the ashtray.

My Mom was born in Pittsburgh and she really did witness Bill Mazeroski's miracle Game 7 home run. She bought the ashtray at Forbes Field, and all these years later gave it to me as an innocent heirloom, a gift, a link to the past. But as these strange apparitions continued to rise up from the ash tray, I began to wonder if maybe it wasn't a gift. I hung in there and faced the chin music. I thought about Ray Chapman, paused for a moment of silence, and then continued on my way.

The baseball fanatics were obviously contacting me through cigarette smoke as a portal into my world. They didn't make weird noises or glow in the dark. That would be too obvious and scare me half-cocked and crazy. I would probably scream and run upstairs and abandon the diamond. My parents would look at each other in some strange pitcher-catcher telepathic way saying it was time to get Dr. Shinko on the horn and call for some bullpen help.

So the ghosts chose a more covert route by appearing only to me and only through soft smoke signals. Maybe I was one of the hidden baseball fanatics? I wasn't sure, but I wasn't imagining things, because I felt a jolt through my system and it turned out to be more than lightning. It was a nudge from the outside. It was Casey Stengel's arm pushing me off the bench and into action. My name was being called, penciled into the lineup. The moment had arrived.

"No time to feel miserly," Stengel said. "You can win. You can lose. Or it can rain." He went on and on about his part-time players making the Ferris wheel spin.

"The American League has no lights," he continued. "We don't mind players from faraway lands. I like a double-breasted suit. You want a pretzel? Go get 'em! Get outta here!"

Mr. Stengel was one confusing double-talker, but the smoke billowed heavily and I watched the wrinkles in his face transform into a crown. It was time to leave the clubhouse and take that long walk up the basement steps and show my face to the world.

What I dreaded more than anything else was the sound my metal spikes might make, tap tap tapping on the tile floor. I dressed in a home Brewers uniform, #33, Rob Deer, and walked west through very anonymous breezes.

"Watch out for tires," Mom yelled from the window. "The burning tires on the highway. Stay away from the revolution. Have fun. Your mother loves you."

I must have walked a long way from home because Wisconsin Avenue soon come into view. I never bothered to check if the Brewers were scheduled to play that afternoon, but I trusted the trees. They whispered everything I needed to know. The first stop was Potawatomie Bingo. It was located down in the Menominee Valley, approximately one Cecil Fielder moon shot away from County Stadium.

Providence was shining on me that golden blue and yellow day because I was greeted at the entrance by a young Winnebago man who eyed me up suspiciously. I knew he was the one. I trusted Native Americans more than any other Americans because I was convinced they understood why a bird might land on a mailbox. It had a deep meaning only a Native American could understand.

He told me to buy a package of Johnsonville Brats, the same ones I heard about on the radio. I was instructed to cook them on a stranger's grill in the County Stadium parking lot.

"Try tailgating on three different grills," he said. "If anyone mentions the name Chief Yellow Horse," he continued, "return home immediately and re-read a History of the Pacific Coast League. There will be a personal message for you on page 285." I knew 285 to be the Atlanta Interstate that swallowed pitcher Pascual Perez for a short while back on August 19, 1982. The Winnebago and I were speaking the same language.

They played rough in the County Stadium parking lot. One guy almost took my hand off and he was just shaking it to say hello. Another guy patted me so hard on the back I nearly fell over, but it was all in good Brewers' fan fun. But no one whispered Chief Yellow Horse, so I didn't return home and reread page 285. I entered the stadium instead. Milwaukee was playing the Chicago White Sox and one of the Sox pitchers kept pointing to the sky after recording a strikeout. I felt like it might happen any moment.

After the 7th inning rendition of "Roll Out the Barrel," a Native American-looking man wearing a Milwaukee Braves hat appeared on the scoreboard. It was a rally cry to commemorate Milwaukee winning the World Series back in 1957. The Native American stayed on the scoreboard long enough to gain eye contact with me. I was convinced it was Geronimo.

I leaped over the 1st base railing and raced towards where I thought Geronimo was running. I was forced to make a detour by strange looking men in blue coats. I was on the outfield grass and heading in the direction of second base. I then turned and raced towards third and began to taste home, but a blue coat grabbed a hold of my shirt. I slipped through his fingers, but blue coats were running towards me from the other direction, counter clockwise, apparently not out of the base line or maybe they were in on the conspiracy. One of them knocked me down and hollered "You're outta here," and dragged me feet first to the White Sox on-deck circle. The rest happened in a swirling siren flash.

The hardest part about prison was finding a pencil and paper. I learned a lot from my cell mate Javier Montafante. He was a big baseball player in Cuba during the Missile Crisis. He learned how to improvise in Havana and we did the same in Milwaukee. We smuggled egg shells outside the breakfast room, hid them in our prison uniforms, and later on dipped them in a compound of toothpaste and Kool-Aid. The sharp edges of the egg shell dipped into the mixture produced a decent writing system. Paper was a little more time-consuming to make. Leaves collected from the yard took sometimes three to four days to dry. We only picked fresh green leaves. They took a lot longer to prepare, but there was less of a crumple factor. I never told Javier what my plan was. He was just glad to kill some time on the production end of the project.

The authorities may have refused to give us pencils for safety reasons, but they never hesitated to provide us Bill James reading material, and so I recreated the entire 1986 Strat-O-Matic baseball season onto our prison-made leaf cards, all the player cards, fielding charts, advanced strategy options, and ballpark adjustment factors. Javier was blown away by Bill James and excited by the numbers coming to life through cards and dice and chance and hell if he was ever going to lose.

He seduced rival prison gangs to join the competition. The waiting list was long, but no one complained. Time was never something we lacked. Rumor became reality. It was true what everyone was saying about on base percentage. There was a hush through the hallways, only the sound of dice on cement and the occasional roar from a walk-off home run. Javier wanted me to make a retro Gene Tenace card. "All those walks," he said, rubbing his hands together.

I studied Bill James abstracts night and day and designed retro leagues so inmates could replicate the season they were born. Violence in the prison vanished. I was praised by both guard and prisoner. They didn't want me to go, but freedom called my name one gray Tuesday afternoon. The inmates were too busy to say goodbye. I had left them under Strat-O-Matic care and control.

The guards rolled their arms in a distinctively eastern direction. So that's the direction I roamed. There would be golden arches somewhere up ahead and when I reached them, I could begin again with a McDonald's coffee.

And there was a McDonald's coffee, and farther ahead a sofa and the smell of incense, too. I had arrived at Dr. Shinko's office and he was glad to see that I loved more than one significant other. I had returned to crown him as my manager.

# Durgy's Home Stand

Jimmy Durgendoff dreamed of being a movie star, then a fire-man, and finally a born again baseball something. I discovered him on Craigslist.

His ad was different from the graphic sex requests or info-mercials announcing an all-in-one broom and mop invention. It simply said, "Vagabond trails, care to meet for a beer at *Cromartie's*?" He also left a phone number.

I was put at ease by his voice. He didn't say good morning or can I help you? He said, "mmmmmnyellow," a mid-western sort of phone greeting. That voice was Jimmy Durgendoff. He had put Craigslist ads in just about every North American city and in each one he invented a place to meet that did not exist. There was no *Cromartie's* Bar on St. Laurent Street in Montreal, not yet anyway, but Warren Cromartie did play for the Montreal Expos from 1974-1983 and in 2012 he created The Montreal Baseball Project in the hope major league baseball would one day return to Montreal.

Jimmy was traveling across country in a Datsun 720 King Cab pick-up truck. I know the specific name and model number because Jimmy began almost every sentence with "King Cab."

It was annoying at first, but I soon understood the qualifier as a jumper cable to rev his mind.

Jimmy is a born again. I'm not sure what he got born again into, but he speaks in gusts that only a shortage of breath slows down. He quit acting after six years of what he calls "whoring for cleaning fluid commercials." He then trained as a fireman and graduated in the top 10 of his class, but that's when he started having visions.

Jimmy's wife wasn't experiencing the same visions. She kicked him out of the house and sent him to the curb, but gave him the keys to her Datsun pick-up truck. Jimmy has been on the road ever since. Jimmy says it was in an uninhabited town on the border of Louisiana and Arkansas where the visions really kicked into gear. He was to be a major league baseball player. Jimmy had never played above junior varsity and was already 37, but this was not a vague flash. The visions came housed in great detail with specific instructions regarding time, location, and contact information.

Jimmy headed north and east, zigzagging his way to tryouts of over two dozen Independent League teams–in Lancaster, Long Island, Lakewood, Lehigh, and Harrisburg. He dug his feet deep in the dirt, stepped out of each and every batter's box, stalled until all eyes were on him and then slapped lazy ground balls somewhere in the infield.

It wasn't until he reached Erie, Jamestown, and further west in Traverse City that he loosened his grip and shook his ass a bit. He held the bat lower and not as stiff, got his hips into the swing and wouldn't you know it! That ball started flying off his bat, whistling line drives into the alleys.

There were second and third call backs, but no contracts, so Jimmy drifted the opposite direction—to the northwest, crossed over into British Columbia, and headed north along the old Chilkhoot trail. It was there where he spotted a moose and its stiff antler rack and wouldn't you know it, bubbling up through Jimmy's mind came another vision!

He was to be a big league pitcher. Jimmy bought a set of antlers and tossed makeshift rings around the pointy ends. His precision and control improved. Jimmy knew all about Christy Mathewson tossing rocks through an eight-pane window and Walter Johnson catching rodents with nothing but tiny pebbles and his bare hands.

Jimmy turned east and retraced the same roads he had taken as a wannabe batter–to Lancaster, Long Island, Lakewood, Lehigh, and so on. We met in Montreal on St. Laurent Street, outside the bar *Cromartie's* that didn't exist, not yet anyway.

Jimmy reeled off one Expos pitcher after another. He wanted to change the name of our fictitious bar from *Cromartie's* to *Cactus Jack* to honor Jack Billingham, the first pitcher selected by the Expos in the 1968 expansion draft.

Jimmy went on and on about how Jack never played for the Expos, about how he was drafted October 14, 1968 and then traded to the Astros on opening day April 8, 1969, about that trade bringing Rusty Staub to Montreal, about Jack being cousins with Christy Mathewson.

It was as if the universe began with Jack Billingham. Jimmy couldn't stop. I didn't want him to. "King Cab," he said. "Billingham was traded to the Reds with Joe Morgan. King Cab! Cactus Jack dominated in the World Series."

Jimmy left me in a cloud of exhaust. He was still talking up a storm as he drove off. I watched the pickup truck slowly turn into a matchbox car and imagined a Jimmy Durgendoff pitch that one day might do the same, a 78 mph vanisher.

I felt strange as the silhouette slipped into the horizon and vanished. There was a loud silence. It was hard to admit, but I missed Jimmy Durgendoff. I combed Craigslist in search of a new distraction, but soon discovered what I already knew. Jimmy Durgendoff could not be replaced. I went to the grocery store and bought beer and peanut butter/chocolate ice cream instead. I watched replays of regular season baseball games from the 1970's.

I began to engage telemarketers like long-lost friends. One voice identified itself as Lawrence Pittman, owner of the Clarion County Sleephogs, a new team in the Diamond Daze Independent Baseball League. The voice sounded young and hopeful, each sentence finishing with a lilt. I couldn't tell if it was a sales pitch or his Irish ancestry. It didn't matter. Mr. Pittman offered me a job with a baseball team.

The team needed a caretaker for its carnival-like speed pitch game, three balls for a dollar, step right up and see how fast you can throw a baseball. I must have emailed a CV to Mr. Pittman. The job was nothing more than a dunk tank cashier, but the position included room and board plus a small salary, not to mention a chance to travel on a team bus. I didn't know what my role would be at away games, but I was living on a friend's couch in Montreal where there was no baseball team. I had nothing to lose, so I packed a bag and walked to the Greyhound Bus station, destination Clarion, Pennsylvania and the 4,000 seat Sleephog Stadium.

The blur of green trees outside the bus window felt fresh and minty. I must have fallen asleep, because when I opened my eyes, there was only one other passenger and Clarion was announced as the next stop, 10 minutes away.

I only had the one bag so I walked four blocks to the stadium. The Sleephogs were holding a practice in preparation for an exhibition game scheduled the following afternoon. Mr. Pittman met me in the main concourse. He looked exactly as he sounded on the phone, small and enthusiastic.

My itinerary was mapped out like a military operation—check into motel, sign employment contract papers, take tour of stadium, and learn how to operate speed pitch. The motel room came with a microwave, fridge, and two stove top burners. The clerk said everything in Clarion was 20 minutes away. I threw my bag on the bed and retraced my steps back to the stadium.

There was a lot of information to gather, nothing too complicated, just a lot of handshakes. I promised Mr. Pittman I would be back the following morning at 9 AM. I showed up 15 minutes early. Mr. Pittman walked me through the speed pitch preparations. The contraption was the size of an 8x12 room, but resting on wheels, making it real easy to push. We set up the cage behind the bleachers. I was given a small tackle box bank, one dollar for three balls no matter what. "We anticipate a dozen or so hard-core drunks every game," Mr. Pittman said. "It's inevitable. Talk to them about the Sleephogs, mention a few players. Try to get the drunks thinking about baseball." Mr. Pittman winked at me so I assumed he was confident I could handle the job. And I was right. After no more than 20 minutes, he put his arm around me and said he had other business to attend to. I watched him walk away, getting smaller and smaller, replaced by a man moving much faster in the opposite direction.

The man had a wiry beard, and as he got closer, he pulled the bill of his Sleephogs hat over his eyes. The sound of metal cleats tap dancing on the asphalt got louder. I tried to move out of the way, but the stranger's arms wrapped around me in a big bear hug and his facial hairs rubbed like steel wool against my cheek.

"How in the hell do you think you got this job?" asked the voice with no intention of waiting for an answer. "King Cab! So it's not the Expos, but it is baseball and you are here and so am I."

My first reaction was "someone forgot to take their medication," but as this guy's grip got tighter, I relaxed a bit and inhaled. There was a distinct smell of beer and patchouli. I began to make sense of it all—Montreal, the pick-up truck, *Cromartie's* on St. Laurent Street that didn't exist, visions. I felt a smile forcing its way onto my face, part nervous and part relief. It was Jimmy Durgendoff. I couldn't speak. This was the greatest thing that could have happened to me. I was excited about getting a job in baseball, the housing accommodations and food money, but I was still alone. I was walking on air.

Jimmy had earned a spot as Clarion's mop up man, but had his mind set on the closer's role. I guess that's why he grew a beard. I never asked. I was too excited to see him. He didn't have time to talk. The exhibition game was scheduled to start in less than an hour, but he told me to join him by the bullpen down the right field line when my speed pitch gig finished.

"Come and see me chew sunflower seeds with the boys in the pen" were Jimmy's parting words. I reached out to hug him, but he had already turned around and was sprinting towards an opening in the home run fence. I watched him run across the outfield grass.

About a dozen fans stopped by speed pitch and everything went well. Mr. Pittman returned and suggested I talk more about the team. "Don't be shy," he kept saying. He handed me a folder filled with reams of information—player profiles, a brief history of the League, statistics, nearby tourist attractions. He instructed me to read up on the team, town, and league before opening day.

"Now go and watch the game and keep your Sleephogs shirt on so everyone can see it." The t-shirt was my uniform/two-sided sandwich board advertisement. The Sleephog emblem was featured on the front and back. I was too happy to feel exploited.

I was excited to see Jimmy and this made the day drag slow, but the 6th inning arrived and the work day done. There were a few empty seats along the right field line. Jimmy was engaged in conversation with one of the other pitchers. He turned to greet me.

"King Cab!" Jimmy yelled so the other pitchers could hear. And when Jimmy was sure everyone was listening, he spoke louder and faster.

"I never did like these open air bullpens. Damn air strips is what they are, hard to tell if we're coming or going. If they're gonna call it a bullpen, then enclose us in a pen for Christ sake."

He pointed towards an imaginary space beyond the home run fence, smiled and said, "That's where a bullpen belongs, out of sight, out of mind."

I took a quick scan at the other pitchers. Most of them were watching the game and not paying attention to Jimmy. Others rolled their eyes.

"Hey princess," Jimmy continued. "How is our holiness today? Did you manicure your nails?"

Princess was Bobby Thornbrooke, the only player who skipped the team bus and drove his own car to all games, home or away. Thornbrooke didn't take Jimmy's comment lightly.

"Shove it Durgy. Shove it up your crazy ass."

"Is something a matter with our pampered princess?" Jimmy asked.

Thornbrooke jumped up, but before the situation could escalate, the other players formed a wall between him and Jimmy. They were apparently used to the routine. Jimmy turned and antagonized a different pitcher.

He had a tailor-made rant against each member of the bullpen. Opening day was scheduled for the following day and I had the sense no one wanted Jimmy on the team, no one in the bullpen anyway. Maybe the position players, coaches, or manager felt differently.

I slept well that night, not the least bit nervous about opening day. Clarion is where I wanted to be. In the morning I moved with the speed and grace of a short order cook. I had a purpose: to get to work on time and meet up with Jimmy after the 6th inning.

Some of the same fans from the exhibition game returned, a little bit drunk as Mr. Pittman had warned, but I was free to speak easy with them. We discussed the Sleephog roster, former Indy League players on major league teams, the price of beer, the Electoral College. It didn't even feel like work.

The game was an offensive explosion through three innings. The Sleephogs scored two runs in each frame and so did the Crablegs from Sussex County. The game was tied 8-8 by the time I reached Jimmy beside the bullpen. He was warming up and called in to pitch to start the seventh inning. It gave me a chance to talk to the other pitchers. Most of them made strange exhale sounds through their teeth or scratched their heads, grateful to be free from Jimmy for a few innings, but they all agreed he could pitch. Jimmy had made the team on the last day of tryouts after throwing close to 100 consecutive pitches for strikes, all corner paint jobs. Barney Skoglin had never seen that kind of precision and control in all his years of managing.

Jimmy worked a 1-2-3 eighth inning, and as I walked around the stadium towards the dugout to speak with him, it dawned on me that Jimmy's vision had really come true. He was a professional baseball pitcher. There were rules and regulations, responsibilities and expectations, a discipline to follow. This was maybe not so easy for Jimmy. This was not the open road.

Jimmy indicated with his hand to hop the waist-high fence and follow him down the dugout tunnel. No one noticed us.

"I love pool halls," he said as we reached the clubhouse. He flung his jersey towards the shower and began to pace. "And I love outdoor concerts and jumping off limestone quarry cliffs and all these baseball bastards." I had become accustomed to Jimmy speaking in random wild gushes, but "so many baseball bastards?"

"Nine positions or 10 if we include the DH," Jimmy explained, "Each one a very unique prototype." Jimmy was sounding so serious and scholarly. He didn't use words like prototype.

"Our pretty boy playboy shortstop," he continued. "Could only be a shortstop. And the goody two shoes, momma's boy second baseman. What about our alpha male catcher and his

Napoleon complex. You already met our Hollywood closer—the Princess, Bobby Thornbrooke."

I noticed him clenching both fists as he sounded out the names of all Sleephog starters. "Bunch of bastards" Jimmy shook his head and sat down. I wanted him to hurry up so we could escape the clubhouse and be on our way before the team arrived, but Jimmy took a shower and by the time he finished, so had the game. A buffalo herd stomped above us. We knew the Sleephogs had won, probably on a walk-off home run in the bottom of the ninth. The sound grew louder as the team made its way through the tunnel and emptied into the clubhouse. There were many conversations going on, all of them very uplifting, and why wouldn't they be? The Sleephogs had indeed just won with a walk-off by the catcher. Jimmy was the only one not laughing. He approached tomorrow's starting pitcher.

"What the hell did you have to do with the win?" he asked, but it wasn't a question. It was an attack. "You could have stayed home and we still would have won. You're a useless son of a bitch four out of five days."

The catcher stepped in between the two of them, but before he could say anything, Jimmy grabbed an imaginary microphone and held it in his hand.

"Do you realize Mr. Mussolini catcher how stupid you look with a pinch for a mustache?" Jimmy stretched out his right hand and was about to touch the pinch when the catcher threw up his right leg and drop kicked Jimmy to the floor.

"The world doesn't need any more pinch stashes," Jimmy yelled on the way down.

The manager Skoglin arrived to the clubhouse and saw Jimmy on the floor and laughed. He had no idea the Kung Fu was real.

I helped Jimmy to his feet and suggested we grab a bite to eat at Tina's Diner. Jimmy either didn't hear or chose to ignore me.

"My God, what a sight you are!" Jimmy said to the third baseman. "I had no idea what a fat ass you were under that baggy uniform. No wonder you can't bend down and guard the line from doubles!"

"Easy there Durgy," said Skoglin. Barney Skoglin was a good-natured skipper, wouldn't hurt a fly. He let the boys have their fun. They could rub magic powder on bats, play poker, or drink beer in their underpants, just as long as they showed up on time.

The Jimmy situation didn't put Skoglin over the edge, certainly not after one game. Skoglin held a soft spot for Jimmy, so did the entire coaching staff. The fact that he was nearing 40 made it even more amazing. Jimmy's three-quarter delivery and circular wind up, his right arm swinging 360 degrees before every pitch, was unique. He didn't throw very fast, but he varied the speed, including a 60 mph change-up that buckled a batter's knees, made his fastball appear like 90. Skoglin sensed my calming effect on Jimmy and called me into his office. We talked a bit about the game, Jimmy's change-up, the local Fracas River, and then Skoglin encouraged me to sit down.

"Listen, I prefer nipping situations in the bud before they go all Jack in the Beanstalk on us, you following? It's the first day of the season," Skoglin explained, "And two players have already come to speak to me about Jimmy. Maybe it's me making mountains out of mole hills, but this old jalopy of mine (Skoglin pointed to his knees) needs to rest. It's a long season. Now please don't argue with me son. I seen all walks of life come into the clubhouse and Jimmy's gotta chance to be here awhile. Take this 500 bucks and do us all a favor."

I didn't give Skoglin a chance to finish.

"You mean like a private stripper?" I asked.

Skoglin laughed. "I was thinking more along the lines of a head doctor, but I like your sense of humor son. The Sleephogs have a team shrink. Maybe he'll prescribe some medication for Jimmy. His office is 10 minutes away."

"What's with the 500 bucks then?" I asked.

"For the trouble it may cause you. Consider it a fetcher's fee. The doctor is paid by the team so you keep the 500, alright? Now get outta here. It's only 3:30 and Dr. Mansfield will be waiting for you."

I took the 500 bucks, thanked Skoglin, and asked him about tomorrow's game, if Jimmy would see any action.

"Never can tell," Skoglin said. "Now git, would ya! Go on! Get outta here! You got two hours. Let's take care of this situation before it goes forest fire crazy on us."

The doctor's office was inside the Clarion shopping mall. It was the last place we thought to look, but after 15 minutes of driving around in circles, we stopped the car and asked a crossing guard. He confirmed that the address was in the mall.

We walked inside and turned left instead of right, in the opposite direction of the doctor. Jimmy spotted a lady sitting at a kiosk holding up a cardboard sign spelling out, *Nuts and Bolts Astrology*. She wore a white apron with as many pockets as a fishing vest.

"She looks close enough to a doctor," Jimmy joked.

"I'll take anything from a pack of cigarettes to a stack of postcards," she said.

Jimmy and I looked at each other and laughed. I pulled out a 10 dollar bill from the wad Skoglin had given me and dropped it on the table. The lady smiled.

"Who's up to bat?" she asked. A good start, I thought, slipping in a baseball reference like that. Jimmy pulled up a chair and placed his hands on the table.

"I need one thing from you," she insisted. "I need a list of people in your life. I need their names written on a piece of paper." Jimmy looked up at me. I liked the way we could communicate without talking. I reached into my bag and found a copy of the Sleephogs roster and handed it to her. She bowed in our direction and asked us to call her Sunbake.

"Turn your hands over, palms up," she instructed. "Close your eyes and breathe slowly. That's it, through the nose." She held the roster over Jimmy's palms and began to read each name very slowly, accentuating each syllable, turning the roster into a song. The last name was Paulino Yulenteeeeeedo.

"Now open your eyes." She snapped her fingers three times. "What year were you born? What month? What time?" The questions arrived one after another, like bullets. Jimmy didn't answer right away. He was rubbing his eyes, readjusting to the light.

"Write down the answers on this paper and hand it to me when you're finished. And you, take this 10 dollars and get me a coffee."

I took the small walk and returned with one black coffee and $8.50 in change. Miss Sunbake bowed to me, scooped up the paper with Jimmy's answers and read them in silence while pacing back and forth 10, 11, maybe 12 times before crashing back down into her chair.

She drew us closer by waving her fingers and then explained a few astrological signs and moons rising with corresponding behavior traits. It was interesting and kind of accurate, but lacked any specifics pertaining to Jimmy's life. Then she leaned back in her chair and pointed directly at Jimmy's chest.

"You've been damaged, hurt real bad. The insults and ridicule began at a very young age. You have brothers and sisters and friends from school that caused you great pain. Maybe you will take a journey or maybe you already have. Yes, you've already traveled many miles to lessen the intensity of this pain, but your past haunts you or the people in your past do. And now you are here and the faces you see are masks reminding you of another time."

She asked Jimmy to turn over his hands again.

"Palms up. This is your life line." She traced a number of different lines and inserted the names of Sleephog players into her speech. "The claustrophobia you feel is real. This is your boxing ring. Fly on and fight!"

And that was it. Jimmy and I wanted to know more, but Miss Sunbake just shrugged her shoulders and smiled.

Some of the same fans dropped by speed pitch the following day. It was Memorial Day, and in Clarion that meant an afternoon doubleheader with an actual marathon between games. The Sleephogs lost the first game, 3-2, a great pitcher's duel. Jimmy motioned with his head for me to hop the fence. We walked across the field. I followed Jimmy into the dugout and clubhouse. He didn't say a word to anyone. He sat beside his locker with head held in hands. The other players looked at me and shrugged their shoulders wondering what was wrong with him.

The catcher cupped his hands together to simulate a megaphone and announced that Jimmy had been medicated and would be well-behaved from now on. Jimmy didn't say a word. I think the astrologer was right. Jimmy was indeed experiencing a flood of flashbacks to his childhood. Sunbake had set free even more memories. The alpha male catcher reminded him of someone and so did the million dollar closer, fat ass third baseman, and so on.

The clubhouse was silent except for the reporters asking questions about the first game. Jimmy didn't bother taking a shower. He removed his uniform and cleats and walked outside in Bermuda shorts and a t-shirt. He didn't say anything as we zigzagged our way through the parking lot.

It was around 3 PM. The marathon had already started. We had three hours to kill before the second game. Jimmy drove slower than usual. Maybe he was being extra careful in case someone from the marathon suddenly rounded a corner. But even after we crossed the Fracas River where there were no runners, he still drove real slow. He looked deep in contemplation. I asked him to park in the back of Tina's Diner. I didn't think it was a good idea for him to be behind the wheel and anyway, I was kind of hungry.

He ordered a stack of pancakes, three sausage links, toast, eggs, and a cherry danish. He took one or two bites and dunked it into a sunny side egg.

"Let's go outside." Jimmy pushed the plate away, stood up and headed for the door. A gust of warm air hit our faces. "Have you ever been north of Montreal?" Jimmy asked. "I always wanted to be a husky dog sled racer."

"The summer hasn't even started," I said. "Are you having another vision?"

"Well, I do love husky dogs," he said "And seeing all that quiet snow, so damn perfect up there in the mountains, all the evergreen trees lining the hillside, all that virgin territory."

We sat down at one of the red picnic tables outside the diner and stared in silence at the river. It split the city into two unequal parts. Jimmy removed a pack of Tiparillos from his back pocket. I had no idea he smoked. Maybe he saved them for special occasions like this, a ceremonial send-off of sorts?

My stomach began to hurt. I was afraid Jimmy's next words might be "nice knowing you, take care, good luck" followed by that painful sight of Jimmy and his King Cab melting into the horizon again. But something much better happened.

Jimmy lit his Tiparillo, and as he did a green car pulled up beside us. I knew it was a Lincoln Continental because of the funky opera windows down the back sides. A grey-haired man with a decent sized belly exited the car, and without saying a word, flexed his thumb. He needed a light. He skipped formal introductions like the elderly sometimes do.

"I roamed sandlots with nothing but a lawn chair, stop watch, a six pack of beer, and this old jalopy. They still call me 'Bird Dog'."

He pointed toward his Lincoln and smiled. "I was one of them boys on the field, a pitcher," he continued. "I never could throw that hard. We never did have no radar guns, but hell if I didn't make batters play the fool, swinging at my change-up, turned 'em all into graveyard diggers, their own grave. Then those radar guns arrived and my confidence nosedived. I traded in my glove for a bar stool and a scout's eye."

He put a Camel in his mouth and tilted his head toward Jimmy who struck a match and lit his cigarette. Bird Dog nodded, sucked three times on the camel, exhaled, and continued.

"I bumped into young men talking big, drinking their drafts, same kind of kids who pushed me out of baseball with their big arms, but I'll tell you this..." Bird Dog put his arm around Jimmy. "I wish I never would have quit. I was better than all of them. That's my big regret. The only thing I'm any good at any more happens around Happy Hour. I'm the only one ready for another. I can drink those aces into the ground."

Bird Dog let out a big belly laugh. Jimmy and I looked at each other and we started to laugh too, and in a few seconds, we forgot why we were laughing in the first place.

"I always preferred the finesse types anyway," Bird Dog continued. "Like me" and then he started with that laugh again and so did we. I tapped Jimmy on the shoulder and whispered so Bird Dog wouldn't hear.

"Maybe Skoglin hired this guy to stalk us, to bring you back?"

"The Sleephogs are playing a doubleheader today," Bird Dog interrupted and "I missed the first game." He had no clue that Jimmy Durgendoff the relief pitcher for the Sleephogs, was who he was talking to.

"They lost 3-2," I said, "Great pitcher's duel."

"Well, there's bound to be some offense in the second game. Why don't you boys join me?" Bird Dog flashed a press pass. "I can get you in for free."

Jimmy took a long look at Bird Dog and a smile came over his face. "I wouldn't mind being like you Bird Dog, holding court at the rail. I wouldn't mind at all."

Jimmy then turned to me and added in a whisper so Bird Dog couldn't hear, "but I'd much rather be a pitcher for the Sleephogs."

It was twilight and light and dark were working together, splashing shadows across the highway. Jimmy and I both sat in the back seat of the Lincoln as per Bird Dog's request. Jimmy never said anything about the road and his great adventure. He talked with Bird Dog about practical things instead, about installing electrical fixtures and changing a car's spark plugs. The old man encouraged Jimmy to change the oil and filters himself.

"Easy as ice cream pie," Bird Dog said. "And a great way to spend some time with your car, get to know her and what not."

When we arrived to the stadium, Bird Dog insisted we join him in the press box. I let Jimmy explain that we worked as speed pitch caretakers, but that we would love to join him after the 6th inning; "when our day's work was done."

"So you're staff members," Bird Dog said; "Nose to the grindstone types. Alright then! I'll see you after the 6th inning! Just tell the usher Bird Dog sent you."

I'm never good with remembering specific dates except the occasional birthdays of family, friends, and a few baseball players, none more astrologically stimulating than Hank Aaron's being February 5th and Babe Ruth's a day later on February 6th. But when I heard Jimmy's name announced as the starting pitcher, I had a feeling this was going to be one of those days.

Jimmy was making the first start of his professional career. I watched him walk out to the mound. He looked calm and determined. He picked up the rosin bag between warm up pitches, inhaling and exhaling in some meditative way I never knew he had in him.

The bleachers began chants of "Durgy, Durgy, Durgy." It sounded like dirge to me as in a mourning song at a funeral, kind of appropriate considering a part of Jimmy had maybe just died, that part inclined to always escape.

I raced down the ramp and into the bleacher concourse. There were a few people waiting in line at speed pitch. I made small talk, took their money, let them throw their pitches, and raced back up to see.

My nerve endings were on fire. The fielders felt close. I could see their twitching fingers and raised toes in case the pinball shot from the cannon and rolled their way. Everyone is supposed to know what to do—gather up the ball, make a clean relay throw, and hope for the best. They've rehearsed it thousands of times, but the real deal is always different. There are shadows and airplane sounds, wind, a player's past, and ghostly distractions that all get in the way.

"Durgy, Durgy, Durgy."

Jimmy walked around the rubber, paying his last respects to the mound before mounting it. I had a good feeling about this. The leadoff batter walked over home plate making sure to not step on it. His batting gloves were perfectly positioned in his back pockets, half in and half out, flapping in the breeze. Jimmy didn't look the least bit impressed. He was fully focused on the catcher flashing signs.

The batter paused outside the box long enough for the crowd to notice and then milked the ceremony some more. He leaned the bat against his crotch and removed the batting gloves from his pocket, slid his fingers into the tight sleeves, and then raised his fists to the sky making sure the fit was snug. He fastened and unfastened the Velcro and then did it again.

This all happened in a matter of seconds under the fading sun and buzzing electric lights, almost at full glare now with a couple thousand eyes looking on, including Bird Dog buried in the press box somewhere.

I raced back down the ramp, relieved to find no line up and no Mr. Pittman checking up on me. I retraced my steps and let my eyes drift towards the bullpen, but not the one down the foul line fully exposed. I imagined the other bullpen, the one

Jimmy liked to imagine, the one tucked away beyond the home run fence out of sight and mind, introverted, where maybe a hot foot ritual was under way.

I let my eyes go back and forth between both bullpens— the real and imaginary— between Jimmy's visions and Jimmy's sweat and determination. My heart pumped an extra beat as the count went full on the first batter. I felt satisfied and walked slowly down the ramp towards the speed pitch cage, and that's where I stayed until the middle of the 6th inning.

I have no idea how I remained so calm with Jimmy on the mound especially with that P.A. announcer saying over and over, "And for the Erie Eagles this half inning, no runs." This went on for six innings and every time, I fled my speed pitch post to take a peak at the scoreboard, to make sure it was true.

Bird Dog was right where he said he would be. He was having the time of his life, happy to see a pitcher with so much precision and control and yet "not a lot of speed, a pitcher just like me," Bird Dog laughed.

I arrived in time to see Jimmy pitch the 7th and did he ever dominate! It was a nine-pitch inning, took no more than five minutes. And the 8th inning was more of the same. Jimmy never took too long between pitches, but this was different. He was in a groove, lost in the flow of the game, moving and pitching in a beautiful rhythm.

Bird Dog and I watched Jimmy walk out to begin the 9th and both of us joined the surrounding chants of "Durgy, Durgy, Durgy." Bird Dog still had no idea that the Jimmy throwing a four-hit shutout was the same Jimmy he had driven to the game. I wasn't about to mess with fortune. The last five hours felt like a dream.

Jimmy walked the first batter and Skoglin strolled slowly to the mound. There was someone warming up in the bullpen, but Skoglin had no intention of removing Jimmy from the game or maybe he did, but whatever Jimmy said must have changed his mind because Skoglin jogged back to the dugout. Jimmy's next pitch was a change-up and the Erie Eagle's batter must have been sitting on a fastball. Bird Dog thought so anyway. He let out a laugh as the ball two-hopped right back to Jimmy who fielded it, spun around, and threw a strike to the second baseman to start a 1-4-3 double play.

Jimmy took his time on the last batter, pausing between every pitch, savoring the end, the final magical moments aloft the mound. After a couple of foul balls on a 2-2 count, Jimmy came back with a change-up for strike three. What a great way for the game to an end, on a swing and a miss!

And what a beautiful sight it was to see Jimmy's teammates crowd around and congratulate him! So many high fives and pats on the ass. All the grudges and hate seemingly forgotten. Maybe they were now believers, too. I jumped up and down and considered storming onto the field, but stayed with Bird Dog instead. He was such a big part of this win, such a big part of Jimmy returning to the team, and he didn't even know it.

We sat and watched the players slide like a collective blob towards the dugout, lingering as the fans made their way to the exits. I asked Bird Dog about the first few innings. He happily provided commentary, frequently returning to his refrain, "Jimmy didn't need a 95 mph fastball, not today or any day, because when the finesse is kicking, it's lights out. It was for me back in the day." And then he would let out that laugh of his, so contagious, and so I started laughing too.

We walked slowly down the ramp, out of the stadium, and across the parking lot. Bird Dog identified the model and year of just about every car. He was like a kid in a candy store. Jimmy was waiting for us in street clothes beside the green Lincoln. Our secret was still intact.

Bird Dog drove us back to where we first met, beside the red picnic tables outside Tina's diner, overlooking the Fracas River. We were once again in the back seat of the Lincoln as per Bird Dog's request. The two of them discussed the different ways to save a broken muffler. Bird Dog suggested inserting a soup can between a split tube and fastening it with metal belts. "Gave my last Lincoln a second chance. She lasted three more years."

I asked Bird Dog to join us for a bite to eat, but his other passion—Miss Dorothy—would be waiting for him. He asked us for a rain check and lowered into his Lincoln, revved the engine, and drove away.

Jimmy and I walked in to Tina's. There were a dozen or so customers sprinkled across the diner. We looked at each other and at the same moment sat down at a table near the front, rather than in one of the big, semi-hidden booths in the back where we normally sat.

The sudden certainty of our move struck me as strange, like we were staking a claim, dropping an anchor. I guess we were. Jimmy had wanted to flee, the way he always does, but he didn't. And I finally had something to hang on to, which I did with gratitude.

Eyeing the napkin dispenser, Jimmy thought aloud, "I wonder if there's a Salvation Army in town." He said he wanted to buy a futon, make Clarion his home.

The next morning we visited apartments and found a decent two-bedroom place overlooking the Fracas River. I had a job with a baseball team and a new roommate. Summer was just beginning and so was Jimmy's baseball career.

# Dreaming .400

There was one package beside Grandpa's bed when he died and it was addressed to me. My name is Sandy Ebbets.

There were only ten people at Grandpa's funeral—three friends, three relatives, and four unknowns. I wasn't one of them, but Grandpa's only son Jerry said the unknowns were "waving crosses and hollerin' all kinds of things."

Jerry spread the worst kind of rumors about his father so this waving crosses stuff came as no surprise, but Jerry explained it all real fast and sounded scared. I could barely make sense of what he was saying.

Jerry didn't come to Pittsburgh to attend the funeral. He came to have first dibs on Grandpa's worldly possessions, but as it turned out, there wasn't much to take and most of it was donated to homeless shelters anyway, except the package.

Albert Marzano was my grandfather from mom's side of the family. He had three children. My mother Gladys was the oldest. Then there was Aunt Myrtle the middle child and Uncle Jerry the youngest and only boy in the family.

Mom waited until Jerry was 2,000 miles out of sight, back to his new home in Reno, Nevada before giving me the package.

She slid the rectangular box across the kitchen table. There was string looped around brown paper in every imaginable direction. I kept tugging, but the string wouldn't budge. It was brown and hairy, a real tough mix of fibers, nearly burned my fingers from pulling so hard. Mom reached into a nearby drawer and pulled out a scissors. She looked at me and without saying a word I pushed the package towards her. She cut through the twine with five or six snips. I think I loved her in that moment more than ever because there it was—the book Grandpa had been reading to me for as long as I could remember.

The cover was still so black and beautiful, plain as can be, starless. Only the spine had marks—three tiny baseballs in yellow ink followed by a straight line and then the words *The Pittsburgh Pirates*, and a second straight line and three more baseballs followed by the author's last name, *Lieb*, and at the bottom of the spine, the word *Putnam*.

I held it tightly to my chest and heat raced through my body, in the tips of my fingers and up my arms and shoulders, down my spine and into my legs, feet, and toes. I jumped up from the kitchen table and imagined the burial ceremony—Grandpa being lowered into some strange dimension where men barnstormed on buses, played baseball in small towns and at night, after another nine innings and scrounging for some grub, listened to Grandpa's stories around a campfire.

The book became a part of my body. I didn't want to put it down, and yet I didn't turn a single page, didn't even open the front cover. I didn't really like to read. It reminded me too much of school, but I always remembered the first time Grandpa held the book in his hands. It was like he was revealing some sacred text, unearthed after 700 years in the ground.

He never read entire pages. He would jump around from paragraph to paragraph and sometimes fly ahead 40 pages, but somehow all the disjointed passages made some strange sense, probably because of the way Grandpa sounded out the second passage as if it was in direct response to the first.

*"Runt from French Creek, NY"* and 35 pages later, *"Half the Pirate team was yipping."*

I was in awe of that book. It took me places I never knew existed, places like Exposition Park and the Fort Wayne Railroad tracks. I learned about players I had never heard of, like Ned Hanlon, "Deacon" Jim White, and Grandpa's all-time favorite, Honus Wagner. There were so many words and expressions I never knew before. Writers were referred to as *scribes*. A response was sometimes called a *snappy rejoinder* and a pitcher might *squelch* the opponent in order in the ninth, getting so and so on an easy *hoist* to right field.

The pages were thick, seemingly made from more durable paper. Grandpa talked often about industries thriving on wear and tear so consumers would spend more money to replace busted parts, "make us all so god damn dependent," he would say.

The Pirates book was different. All those years of being opened and closed, the pages turned and ruffled and it was still in near perfect condition. And inside was a history, a Pittsburgh Pirates history, "and for us baseball fans," Grandpa used to say, "a team history has that extra element. All the players and memorable seasons, or not so memorable ones, could turn a casual fan downright fanatical, and the way Mr. Lieb wrote with so many stories and colorful expressions, well, a book like that was like medicine my boy."

I never had too many books on my shelf. There was "Greatest World Series Thrillers" by Ray Robinson, The Baseball Encyclopedia, a short biography of Joe Namath, and a few letters from the World Book Encyclopedia set. My brother and I split up the alphabet. He got G-Z, 18 books to my 6, but I got the better deal with A-F because B is for baseball and basketball and F for football.

I was the only one in our family who loved baseball and the only one who loved Grandpa Albert. He made it very clear that one day the Pirates book would be mine and I never told a single soul because Grandpa asked me not to.

We moved around a lot because Dad never had enough money so the only place I ever called home was Pittsburgh and Grandpa's two bedroom house. It was small, but we had a TV, a big radio, a back yard, and the eastern sky. It was the same house Mom grew up in and not too far from where Forbes Field used to be. Grandpa and I walked over there a few times, but he preferred taking me to the railroad tracks in Schenley Park. He always asked me to never tell Mom. "Wouldn't want her thinking you might grow up to be like me."

"And how are you?" I would ask.

"Well, some think I'm a good-for-nothing hobo stink and maybe they're right, but once you get that wander feeling, it's hard to stop."

Grandpa called train cars *bodies*. I never doubted his word when it came to trains or baseball, because when he was a kid-baseball players traveled from New York to Pittsburgh by train. There were no airplanes and most of the cars were the kind that sputtered along dirt roads.

It was the beginning of May when Mom handed me the book. There were still two months of school remaining, but the days were already longer and that made me restless, especially after dinner. That's when the urge to roam around was strongest.

There was still some daylight so I put the book in my backpack and walked to the up and down slope behind the grocery store. I wandered through the fallen trees and trash and found a log to sit on. There were no trains passing, but I could see the tracks on the other side stretching in both directions. I pulled out the book, rubbed its cover, and an amazing thing happened. I heard a voice.

"Call me snakeskin," it said. "Go ahead," the voice repeated. "Come on. You can do it. Call me snakeskin." It was definitely Grandpa.

It was getting dark, but I swear I saw him standing on the other side of the slope. He was crouched down on one knee and wearing a baggy Pirates uniform and I knew exactly what he was doing. He was waiting for Honus Wagner to finish his at bat at Forbes Field.

Grandpa was the personal bat boy for the "Flying Dutchman." That's what he always told me anyway. He could never figure out why they called him the "Flying Dutchman" since Wagner was German, not Dutch.

Grandpa talked about Wagner's hands more than anything else, how big and calloused they were, but then he would get real quiet and say, "The closest he ever got to .400 was .380. That was in 1900 before Forbes Field even existed, before I existed."

I felt kind of spooked and ran all the way home and was out of breath as I told Mom how I had seen Grandpa in a Pirates uniform at Forbes Field and that he had talked to me and asked me to call him "snakeskin."

She dropped her glasses to the tip of her nose, squinted her eyes, and smiled. "Come on sweetheart. This is the voice of reason you're talking to, your mother."

I put the book on the table and was surprised when Mom placed her own hand on the book's cover, just like I had done at the up and down slope. I didn't know if she was mocking me or believed the book had magical powers too. One thing was for sure, when she touched the book, she got the urge to speak.

"He sure did love your Aunt Myrtle, used to dance with her like she was a queen. Grandpa taught us both how to Polka you know, not an easy dance to learn." Mom stood up and offered her hand. She wanted to show me the dance, but I wanted to know something else.

"Are you older than Myrtle?" I asked.

"Yes, five years older," Mom said, "But no one could tell the difference. We were best friends. We were so happy when your Uncle Jerry was born. He was like our little son."

I had never heard the entire story about Jerry. It was Grandpa's little secret I guess or something he never got around to telling me. Mom put her hand on the book again, but this time she paused like she was taking an oath. She smiled and I trusted that smile. She wasn't mocking me at all.

"Jerry was born the first warm day in 1968," Mom continued. "Not much different from today, not a cloud in the sky and perfect temperature, right around 65 degrees. Good sleeping weather, and you know what else Sandy?"

I shrugged my shoulders.

"Jerry was born the same day as the Pirates home opener, April 17, 1968." Mom fell silent after saying the date. We just sat there for a while. She eventually put her hand on my shoulder and continued.

"That's the same day your grandmother, Ethel Marzano, died from complications while giving birth."

Mom said "Grandpa returned to the only other family he knew—tramping from town to town and living under the stars, making fires in garbage cans, catching and cooking road kill, sleeping in train yards, bathing in the river, and more than anything else, riding those rails and racing ahead towards tomorrow."

I didn't really understand what all that meant, but Mom also told me that she was 16 years young when she became like a mother and a father to Jerry. That I understood.

Mom picked up the book, handed it to me, and disappeared into the kitchen. I flipped open the front cover, scanned a few pages, and quickly closed it. I had never opened it before, not without Grandpa. I decided to play our game of asking a question and turning to a random page for the answer.

"Will anyone ever hit .400 again?" I asked loud enough so the book could hear, and don't remember the page I flipped to, but I copied the passage word for word on the back of some scrap paper.

*"In 1920 the club also purchased an infielder who was destined to become one of Pittsburgh's all-time greats, Harold Joseph "Pie" Traynor. Both Boston clubs had given young Pie the bum's rush when he tried to convince their respective managers that he was a ball player, yet Traynor became baseball's greatest modern third baseman."*

I looked up Traynor in the Baseball Encyclopedia and he never hit .400, but he did hit .366 in 1930 and that seemed pretty damn close to me.

It was getting late and my eyes were closing and opening. I was slipping between awake and dream. I put the book on my chest and stretched out flat on my back and started thinking about a game no one would probably ever play. I called it Wall Ball.

There was no school the next day. I could sleep until 2 in the afternoon if I wanted. Mom was at work, but I woke up early anyway, wanting to get back to my imaginary world of Wall Ball.

I pushed open the screen door and took a big whiff of spring air and realized there was no need to wander towards the up and down slope. I didn't need the fallen trees and railroad tracks to imagine Wall Ball so I sat down in our back yard, on plain grass, and opened the book to where it was thickest, where there were pictures. I landed on page 276, a black and white photo of Ralph Kiner completely surrounded by darkness. He looked like he was standing on the moon.

I remember Grandpa gushing over Kiner's 51 home run season in 1947, "transformed left field at Forbes into Kiner's corner," he said. I later learned it was the first of five consecutive years Kiner hit 40 or more, a massive explosion, maybe the most ever in such a short span.

Grandpa used to whisper the name Kiner if I ever said the words *can't* or *impossible*, as a reminder. Grandpa didn't believe in *can't* or *impossible*.

I flipped to the last few pages. They were blank. I reached into my front pocket, surprised to find a pen because I never carried one, never needed to. I didn't like to write, but on this day my hand lowered onto the page and began to move on its own. Kind of scared me. I dropped the pen like a hot potato and thumbed backwards through the book, landing on page 278 and as I read, the words soothed me. I felt safe again.

*"Two likable and deserving newcomers made the team that year, Al Gionfriddo, a pint sized Italian outfielder from Dysart, Pennsylvania and Bill Salkeld, a catcher."*

Grandpa typically jumped around when reading, but I was interested by these "newcomers" so I read on.

*"Al, released from the army early in 1944 could scamper around the bases like a jack rabbit and in 122 games hit .284, the same as big Russell. The bobby soxers adopted little Al as their own and greeted him with the same squeals their sisters gave Frankie Sinatra when the crooner broke into song."*

And the next paragraph began with, *"Salkeld, one of the few Idaho boys to make the majors, had a real Horatio Alger story."*

My brain was sizzling. How could so much information and wonder be packed into three small sentences—the *jack rabbits, bobby soxers, Frank Sinatra, crooner, Idaho boys, Horatio Alger* and to top it all off, a delicious *.284 by Al Gionfriddo.* I think that was the same Gionfriddo who robbed DiMaggio of a World Series home run. Grandpa once showed me a picture of DiMaggio kicking up a dust storm of frustration while rounding second base.

I lowered the pen back onto the page and letters formed into words and sentences and paragraphs. I heard Grandpa's voice again, "Go ahead. Come on. You can do it," but this time he didn't say "Call me snakeskin." He said, "Be the snakeskin."

I began to write and couldn't stop. I invented everything. I breathed existence into players and they played Wall Ball.

It began with an abandoned flour mill in right field. I made it tall and wide, at least 40 feet high with tons of broken windows towards the top. On the bottom I added a faded Hergshire and Sons sign with a tomboy-like lady threshing wheat below the company letters. A towering skyscraper blast that cleared the roof, out of sight, would not be just a home run. It would be "Flour Power!"

Was I remembering details described in the Pirates book, passages read to me by Grandpa? I didn't think so because I had never heard about a field like that. I tried not to think and just let my mind flow. The pen followed.

In center field I included a fenced-in area that some would believe to be an old-fashioned water well, 30 feet deep into the earth. Others would insist it was a catacomb and wouldn't dare to enter. To hit a ball there would require carnival-like strength, a 450-foot blast. But in left field there wouldn't be a fence at all so balls could roll for triples and inside the park home runs.

The bases were not 90 feet apart, but close enough. The infield wasn't smooth, lots of broken glass and small pebbles. There were also patches of raised grassy mounds between second and third. Looked like a snake swallowing a rat. I had completed the baseball earth and architecture. Time to turn my attention to the players. I made Skids Royce the best pitcher in Wall Ball and made him as irreverent as they come.

Seconds after I had written Skids Royce on the page, a very spooky thing happened, nearly caused me to throw the pen down and run for the brightest lit room in our house. I heard a stranger's voice in my head that identified itself not as Grandpa, but as Skids Royce.

How was this possible? Characters in books talk to each other, not to the author. Well, Skids or whoever or whatever this was didn't stop screaming so I had no choice but to deal with him.

It was Skids alright and he was behaving like a spoiled brat. Here I gave this guy a life, only a fictional one, but better than nothing, and what does he do? He bitches and complains, says he wants to be the league's greatest hitter, not a pitcher. He wants to hit 80 home runs in Wall Ball's first season. I told him a number like that wasn't even realistic in whiffle ball, but Skids begged and even bribed, saying he would accept striking out 150 times if I would just write him 80 home runs into the script.

Skids was stirring a part of me I never knew existed, one determined to stay the course and not waver. I made Skids a pitcher and dammit, he was going to stay a pitcher!

I must have named him Skids Royce for a reason, to combine opposites—skid row and rolls royce—perhaps because I had a feeling we were going to be friends in a love/hate, generate lots of friction sort of way. He would provoke me and I would provoke him. We would inspire each other. We already had.

Skids argued that I "wronged" him by making him a pitcher and that I would one day pay for it. I slowed the pen down to a molasses pace, in need of a change.

I turned my attention towards Demitri Robinson, a batter, and decided he would flirt with a .400 average during this inaugural Wall Ball season. I felt a secret joy in doing this and Skids must have sensed it because I heard voices screaming again in my head.

"It's easy to reach .400," Skids yelled, "But a real pain in the brain to maintain it, and Robinson doesn't have a chance in hell with me on the mound!"

I put down the pen and wondered where in the world Skids and Demitri came from? My mind of course, but why? Did they remind me of Jerry and Grandpa's dueling banjos as father and son, or were Skids and Demitri warring sides within me?

I would love to hit .400 in any league. That would change my life forever, but being a pitcher and spoiling a batter's attempt might be even better. It could give me an edge, to never back down from anyone.

I flipped pages in any direction and trusted the results like someone lost in the desert would rely on the stars above. I landed on page 155:

*"In the early evening Barney Dreyfus provided grog and fancy victuals to his swashbuckling Buccaneers and the town's sports scribes......."*

I wasn't sure what *grog* and *victuals* or *swashbuckling* were but they definitely lightened my mood, reassured me that Skids and Demitri would survive no matter what the pen and I decided and that I would survive too.

I let the season roll on in my mind, and as it did, I felt Skids and Demitri inside me like the tick and tock of a grandfather clock. But there was nothing playful in the pendulum's swing. It felt more like a tug of war or two trains screaming through the night destined to crash. I flipped to page 101, Honus Wagner at the 1903 World Series, game one, Pittsburgh Pirates versus the Boston Americans in Boston.

*"Hey Dutchman (Honus Wagner) we're going to give you and the Pirates a licking you'll never forget."*

*Honus only guffawed. "Who with?" he asked. "With that old man; Cy Young? Why, we chased him out of the National League years ago."*

That passage made me wonder if this kind of tension maybe existed in everything, if it was necessary to put things in motion. The pitcher played mind games with the batter and cat and mouse with the base runner. Fans ramped up their fanaticism in parking lots, taunting and razzing each other. All the psych-outs and doing whatever it takes to triumph over the opposition. Skids versus Demitri played itself out in countless ways all over the world and inside human hearts, inside my heart. I pushed Demitri's average up to .423 and flipped to page 163:

*"The season of 1912 brought forth Pittsburgh's last great club of the Clarke-Wagner era. While the Pirate runner-up finished ten games behind the champion Giants, it was an exciting, nerve-tingling season for Forbes Field fans."*

*"Nerve tingling"* indeed, and so I dipped Demitri's average below .400 with only three games remaining and then I spiked it above and then below and above and below, right up until the last game. I felt dizzy so I gave the pen and my mind a rest. I wandered inside and sat at the kitchen table and thought about Honus Wagner never hitting .400 and how that bothered Grandpa.

There was never any rhyme or reason to where I turned in the Pirates book, but wherever I landed, the words set Wall Ball back in motion. I thumbed backwards and forwards, arriving this time on page 212.

*"The Pirates felt pretty sick when the Sunday game of October 11 was over. ...The Washington pitching prince, Walter Johnson, once more was supreme, and the Pirates again*

*looked like meek landlubbers, trying to connect with the veteran's fast ball.*"

Could there be a clearer sign? The *pitching prince supreme* was an obvious rally cry for Skids. Had he somehow manipulated my fingers to land on this page 212? Impossible! I created Skids. He had no free will of his own, but maybe my loyalties were clouding my judgment and altering Wall Ball's imaginary destiny?

I liked Skids. Sure, he was loud and aggressive and never took no for an answer and probably caused kids to sleep with stuffed animals. But he had guts and loved a good, old fashioned fight. Demitri, on the other hand was soft and managed to remain out of the spotlight despite knocking on .400's door. He was the sort that gathered up good kindling and left it in the fire pit for tomorrow's camper. I liked him too.

Mom would be home from work soon so I decided to wait and share with her my dilemma—Skids or Demitri—to hit .400 or to not hit .400. I paced back and forth in the kitchen, and when Mom arrived, she smelled trouble like body odor in an elevator, and good thing too because I needed some help. I told her about the Wall Ball world I had created and how maybe the book was...

She interrupted me and said, "You've bitten off more than you can chew." She walked to the front room and peeled back the curtain. I followed behind. We looked out the window together.

"Go visit Grandpa," she said. This was not a suggestion. It was an order.

The cemetery was 10 minutes away by bus and the sun a good three or four hours from setting. I found a window seat and watched places Grandpa once showed me pass in a beautiful but sad blur—the Monongahela River, all those oak trees, and then, there it was, The Allegheny Cemetery.

The hillside was covered with tombstones. The welcom center provided a map. I found Grandpa's name, walked to his burial plot, and sat down. The grass was warm. I closed my eyes and told Grandpa about Skids and Dimitri and my confusion. It felt strange talking to a cement slab, but I continued, because the more I talked the more Grandpa came into focus.

He never answered any of my questions, but I felt my mind slowing down. I opened to the back of the book. One or two blank pages remained. I reached into my pocket for the pen and began. The score was 8-0 in the bottom of the ninth, last day of the season, a meaningless at bat, but a base hit by Demitri would push his average above .400 and carve his name into the forever books. Skids, of course, had something else in mind.

He stepped off the rubber, then back on, then off and on and off again. He reached for a popsicle stick in his back pocket and sat in the lotus position beside the mound just like I was sitting beside Grandpa's tombstone. Skids cleaned dirt from his spikes and stepped back on the rubber.

He shook off a few more signs from the catcher and then went into his wind up and...what's that? What happened? The ball was suspended in mid-air, frozen in space 30 feet from home plate! Skids and Demitri slipped out of their uniforms and disappeared! The entire scene went blizzard white! I shook the pen, but still nothing. The river had run dry. There was no more ink.

I balanced the empty pen carcass on top of Grandpa's tombstone and laughed for the first time since Skids and Demitri were born in my mind. I felt like hugging the tombstone, but touched it with my open palm instead and retraced my steps to the bus stop. It was the middle of May. My friends would be at the playground. I had a bat and a bag of balls at home and there was an almost perfect wall at the school yard.

It didn't have a faded Hergshire and Sons sign like in my Wall Ball story. It was only our elementary school, a red brick building, but it did make an ideal home run wall, and in center there was a fenced-off area that was probably close to 500 feet from home plate.

We would make up teams, set a schedule, and play a full Wall Ball season and I was going to be on the Pirates and relax my back elbow and add some tango to my hips. Summer hadn't even started. Anything was possible.

On the bus ride home, I opened up the Putnam Pirates book and began to read on. This time I didn't flip to a random page. I started on page 1.

*"As far back as the post-Civil War period, Pittsburgh and the surrounding country has been a hotbed of baseball enthusiasm."*

Quotations in this story come from *The Pittsburgh Pirates by Frederick G. Lieb*, Van Rees Press, New York, 1948.

# Close Encounter

February delivers unexpected warm whispers. They slip under pant legs. Squinting stops. The booger freeze melts. No one runs for cover. Minds light up like a 777 jackpot. The animal kingdom slows down. Humans loiter in street corner conversation.

There are flashes of bare feet and beer bottle beaches. Cinderella is ready to be reborn. Every baseball team's record sits at a perfect 0-0.

The sensation haunts Sam Doobins. He cringes at men and women removing animal furs and feathers, at ankle flesh being subtly exposed. He crawls back into the franchise's early years, the Milwaukee Brewers beer barrel logo, its wood spout for a nose and no expectations.

Sam sips beer and watches garbage men move with Nascar pit crew efficiency. He sees the Lynwood girls playing hopscotch in the snow. He observes from behind a sealed bedroom window. The mouths on the street move, but don't say anything, just the way Sam likes it.

Sam remembers being with his father as a five-year old, behind Milwaukee's VA Hospital, atop Mockingbird Hill. It was there where father taught son how to peer into County Stadium's right field, to catch a glimpse of the Milwaukee Braves, for free.

Sam remembers the equipment trucks in the spring of 1970 fleeing Arizona and turning right and not left, heading northeast, not northwest, towards Milwaukee, not Seattle, to become the Brewers, not the Pilots.

Sam remembers sitting atop that same Mockingbird Hill to watch the Brewers, for a few years anyway, until the County Stadium architects suffered ambition and expanded the bleachers and suddenly the Mockingbird view was gone.

Sam suffered through the early years, the nine consecutive losing seasons, but then Bambi's Bombers and 200 home runs happened, a winning record six years in a row, a World Series in 1982, followed by momentum switching directions again, a three-year spiral, but then, oh then! Sweet and miraculous then! The spring of 1987 happened and life was never the same for Sam Doobins. The proof he never asked for appeared in spring flesh. Sam had just turned 27.

On Easter Sunday, April 19, the Brewers hosted the Texas Rangers. They had already won 11 games in a row to start the season, but Sam Doobins wanted more and he wasn't alone in his greed. The Brewers trailed 4-1 in the bottom of the ninth and 30,000 fans remained in their County Stadium seats waiting for a miracle.

The sun was shining, but it was barely 50 degrees and a 15-20 mph wind made it feel even colder. Fans removed their shirts anyway, but not Sam. He huddled under the fleshy mass to perform a magic ritual in secret: tap the right side of his seat four times, pound left foot two times, clap hands and hold them together six seconds.

Glen Braggs walked, and so Sam Doobins tapped, pounded, and clapped. Greg Brock singled; tap, pound, clap. Cecil Cooper flied out to center field. Rob Deer crushed a Greg Harris curve ball into a 20 mph wind, but the ball refused to slow down, soaring to the top rows of the left field bleachers and nearly leaving the stadium. Game tied 4-4; tap, pound, clap.

Sam had never heard so many screams or seen so many people jumping up and down, not even after the last out of the 1982 American League Championship.

B.J. Surhoff struck out. Jim Gantner walked; tap, pound, clap. Dale Sveum hit a high fastball off the same Greg Harris, this one to right field, way less mammoth than Deer's, but enough to clear the fence. The Brewers won 6-4 and no one exited the stadium; tap, pound, clap.

It was too loud to leave, maybe louder than any regular season game Sam had ever attended and it was only April 19th, 12 in a row to start a season; tap, pound, clap.

George Webb never promised free hamburgers. The owner of the Wisconsin burger chain simply predicted the minor league Milwaukee Brewers would win 17 games in a row in the 1940's, just like he predicted the Milwaukee Braves would win 12 in a row in the 1950's, and the major league Brewers the same, and then in 1987 it really happened. The Brewers did win 12 in a row and George Webb must have been feeling generous because the restaurant did more than say "we told you so Milwaukee." It dished out 168,194 hamburgers for free.

Sam Doobins entered the George Webb on Farwell Avenue, April 20th, 1987 at 4:30 pm, approximately 24 hours after Sveum hit his game-winning home run. He sat at a 1950's style booth, fingered nervously with the salt and pepper shakers, and when he was absolutely certain no one knew he was there, he tapped the right side of the seat four times, pounded his left foot two times, clapped his hands and held them together for six seconds.

A skinny-armed waitress slid slowly across the floor and delivered a hamburger to Sam Doobins. Not a word was spoken between them. Sam enjoyed the complementary hamburger in approximately three-and-a-half bites, but an empty feeling came over him as he licked the last chunk of gristle between his two front teeth.

The Brewers were en route to Chicago for game number 13 of the 1987 season so Sam did what any Brewer fanatic would have done. He boarded a Greyhound bus and 90 minutes later stood outside Comiskey Park, scalped a ticket, and watched the Brewers come from behind and beat the White Sox for their 13th win in a row. The streak tied the Atlanta Braves for the all-time record to begin a season, but that's where it ended because the following night Sam watched Chicago defeat Milwaukee 7-1.

Sam arrived home at 2AM and walked to the same George Webb Restaurant which thankfully never closed. He sat at the same table and noticed a strange and annoying buzz from the light bulb above him. It was a sound Sam didn't notice two days earlier when the Brewers were 12-0. He felt frustrated because the Brewers were not going to be 162-0. All his little aches and pains reappeared.

Sam wondered why he had to wear glasses and why they cost so much. But at the same time, he was grateful to not be eating TV dinners and hearing that metal fork scrape across the aluminum tray. That sound reminded him that he was alone.

The same skinny-armed waitress slid slowly across the floor. Sam wanted to ask her a question, but slipped into a monologue instead. "The average lifespan of humans is maybe too high," he said. "The hunters and gatherers didn't last long in terms of years, but they squeezed a hell of a lot in a short time and they never had to bother with gum disease, root canals, and what not."

Sam paused and looked down at the carpet, "But the booths here are cushioned and the pickles crispy," he added. The waitress began to say something, but swallowed her next word and smiled instead.

She had been serving Sam for over a month. Sam thought about her, but only when inside the restaurant. That changed after Rob Deer and Dale Sveum hit Easter Sunday home runs. Sam began to notice a pleasant curve in the corner of her mouth and that she walked with a sort of hippety-hop in her step, always pushing off her toes. He liked the rhythm. Sam began to think about her while at home watching TV.

Sam arrived at George Webb every Monday at 6 PM and the same waitress served him two hamburgers and a Coke. It was their little connection and no one else cared except the night shift manager. He encouraged the waitress to talk more to Sam who began feeling a new kind of hunger, one not satisfied by hamburgers, so he added Thursday at 6 PM to his ritual. This went on for an entire year and their conversation was always pleasant and a few shy smiles were shared, but nothing more.

The waitress had no idea March 21, 1988 was the one-year anniversary of Sam walking into her life, but only because she didn't keep track of time. Sam, on the other hand, knew full well because he recorded notes about each and every day of his life in a little journal.

Take February 27, 1988 as an example:

> *Woke up late, called in sick to work. Ate Tombstone Pizza for lunch, browsed spring training Brewers news in the Milwaukee Journal. Walked to the Ben Franklin Variety store on Oakland Avenue, bought a bottle of Mr. Clean, scrubbed the bathroom floor and fell asleep in the middle of the afternoon listening to the Electric Light Orchestra.*

Sam didn't know too much about astronomy but he knew the earth required 365 days to travel around the sun. It was facts and science and Sam loved those kinds of absolutes like he loved the way the big weeping willow tree leaned over the Milwaukee River, its branches caressing the water like fingertips. Sam felt safe and secure and never hesitated to lay flat on his back and float because the tree always felt so near. But with the skinny-armed waitress in his life, things started to change. The new and unfamiliar sensations he was feeling were reflected in his daily notes. There was no mention of what he ate on March 20, 1988, no play by play of his activities or description of items bought at the Ben Franklin. The only note Sam scribbled was "Life under water feels incredibly strange."

The anniversary night began like any other. It was Wednesday and not Thursday when Sam sat down, but the waitress, not being too good with remembering days of the week either, just assumed it was Thursday.

Sam took a deep breath and resisted the urge to tap the right side of the seat four times and so on. This was a conscious choice on his part. He stood up and stared at the light bulb above his head instead.

He felt brave staring directly into the light, risking retina damage and what not. It was like walking barefoot across hot coals in some ancient courting ritual, and as the skinny-armed waitress neared, Sam began to speak.

"After the initial sting from staring so long," Sam explained, "The purples and blues and aqua marines and twisted helix shapes appearing inside the bulb are ones I've never seen before. They're rather amazing and beautiful."

Sam turned away from the light and watched sparkles appear and disappear under the waitress's eyes. There was blush on her cheeks, but not from make-up. She was used to all kinds of strange behavior. She liked it. That's why she worked at night. That's why she liked Sam.

Sam still didn't know her name and she didn't know his, but the temperature was rising between them. She dropped one of her socks a quarter inch, exposing her ankle, and tucked strands of brunette hair behind her ear. Sam felt himself heating up and scanned the room in search of an emergency exit.

"If I go to Roswell, New Mexico," he said, "I'll go for the same reason many people go, to see a UFO and experience a close encounter, but I'll bring a gym bag and a secret. I'll know the name of the only major league baseball player ever born there."

The waitress already had the green light from her boss. "To let things escalate" were his exact words, so she slipped softly into the booth on the opposite side of Sam. She didn't know much about baseball, but under the table her toes curled up inside her shoes. She studied Sam's profile while folding a napkin into a triangle.

"Was this baseball player an alien?" she asked in a playful manner.

Sam looked left and right to make sure no one was listening and whispered,

"It's like he's carved into my memory. He comes to life in light bulbs and puddles after rain storms, in the shapes of clouds. He keeps me company. He haunts me."

"Did you ever meet him?" she asked.

"Well, not yet," Sam said. "Not in any formal handshake sort of way, but whenever I have him in mind, amazing things happen. Remember the Brewers winning streak last year?"

"I didn't see the game, but I served some free hamburgers, including one to you." She tilted her head.

"Well, I was at that game," Sam said, "and before Deer and Sveum hit those home runs, I sneaked a peak at the mug shot of Marshall Lefty Scott. I have it right here."

Sam reached into his back pocket and removed a passport-sized photo of Mr. Scott and handed it to the waitress. And as she looked at the photo, he continued to speak.

"There he is. Marshall Lefty Scott, born in Roswell, New Mexico and died in Houston, Texas. You can keep the photo. It's for you. Isn't it something?" Sam asked. "No discernible mouth or ears and no identifiable symbol on his hat."

There were a few seconds of silence and then she said, "He does look like an alien. Maybe he was part of some government baseball experiment? Maybe he's not really dead."

Sam looked at the waitress and for the first time didn't pull away.

"What's your name?" he asked.

"Candice, but just call me Candy, and your name?"

"Sam. Sam Doobins, and that's what you can call me."

The waitress had done a lot of reading about Roswell and UFO sightings and ancient civilizations building runways for alien spaceships, but she let Sam speak instead.

"Marshall Lefty Scott threw 22.1 innings and allowed 29 hits, 12 walks and 11 earned runs. He started two games for the Philadelphia Phillies and lost both of them and none of that really matters, but what does matter is that he pitched for three and a half weeks, from June 15, 1945 to July 12, 1945 and that was it. He never pitched again."

"I could build an entire baseball league with all the waitresses and dishwashers that have quit after three-and-a-half weeks," said Candy. "I wonder where they all go."

"But wait a second," Sam said. "Two years later, an unidentified flying object crashed near Roswell, "sometime in June or July" 1947, almost 2 years to the day Lefty Scott walked off the mound for the last time. We're talking about engineers with measurements and pressure gauges, not to mention historians who love dates and yet all they came up with was "sometime in June or July." The vagueness is kind of delicious, don't you think?"

"Like my paper napkin Bermuda triangle?" asked Candy while handing her origami gift to Sam. "What will you do when you get to Roswell?" she asked.

"I'll arrive downtown by bus," said Sam, "and then wander past the tourist shops towards a local diner and order some coffee and toast. The waitress won't smile like you and that will be fine because I'll want to get down to brass tacks."

"Brass tacks?" asked Candy. "That sounds painful."

"Not painful," said Sam, "Just rolling up my sleeves and doing my job."

"And what exactly will that be?"

"Searching for a close encounter," said Sam.

Candy was excited to hear Sam say the actual words *close encounter*. It made her feel wanted.

"I'll wander outside Roswell," Sam continued. "And if tree branches take on strange, impossible shapes and melt into clouds to make even stranger shapes, I'll remain determined and committed."

Candy's toes began to curl again under the table.

"I'll see some kids walking across a field and they'll be carrying a baseball bat. I'll know it's a bat because the sun will hit the aluminum and let out a strange and powerful reflection—one I will recognize from my little league days. The distance between the kids and me will vanish very quickly, and without my saying a word, one of them will ask me if I'm a pitcher."

"I'm a left fielder," I'll say, and then I'll ask the kid if his name happens to be Lefty. He'll shake his head and say, "No, but I pitch left-handed."

"I won't stay long in Roswell, maybe two or three days. I'll play baseball with those kids and at night walk up Gallinas Peak and I won't see a UFO or Lefty Scott or have a close encounter, but the bus ride home will take more than two days and I'll see mountain peaks melt into grassy mounds followed by flat earth and I'll suddenly know."

"Know what?" Candy asked.

"As the bus pulls into Milwaukee's station, I'll know where my next trip will be."

"And where will that be?" asked Candy.

Sam reached for some water and then looked into Candy's eyes. Something terrified him. It was something warm like a quilt in the dead of winter. He quickly changed the subject.

"Imagine mass production as a Neolithic craze," Sam said, "farming hoes and grain silos replaced a hunter's bow and arrow. The La-Z-Boy couch waited in the wings."

Candy liked murder mysteries and reading between the lines. She nodded her head so Sam would continue.

"I lacked self-control when I was a kid and built a kingdom of hats, posters, and baseball emblems, but only a photo of Chief Noc-a-Homa has lasted until this day."

"Chief Noc-a-Homa?" Candy asked. "What tribe is he from?"

"The Milwaukee Braves tribe," Sam said. They were the baseball team in Milwaukee before the Brewers. They played at County Stadium too. Noc-a-Homa lived in the bleachers with one foot inside a tepee and the other one dancing after a Braves home run, and when the Braves moved to Atlanta so did the Chief."

Sam reached into the same pocket he had retrieved the Marshall Lefty Scott photo and pulled out a folded up photo of the chief in full headdress. He handed it to Candy.

"You can keep the photo. It's for you. Isn't it something?" Sam asked. "It was handed down from my grandpa to my father and finally to me and I guard it like a wedding ring, rabbit's foot, and compass all rolled into one. It's just a black and white, but the sway in a dance needs no color. Can you see it? That sway?"

Candy brought the picture close to her face and immediately remembered the tree stumps dotting her Mom's country lawn.

"I used to rub tree rings as a kid. I was trying to set them free and then I would dance."

Candy began to slide her arm across the table, towards Sam, but pulled back a bit when Sam began to talk.

"Grandpa received offers for the Chief's photo. I was the first one to take an interest in the man under the headdress. Levi Walker Jr. was his name. He was the third of the Noc-a-Homa's, I think, born in Ottawa, Canada, a member of the Odawa tribe."

"Nothing but a mascot, don't you think?" asked Candy. "A little like Disney Land, a stuffed animal sort of thing."

Candy sensed that Sam had something important to say so she cupped her hand into the shape of a microphone and placed it under his mouth.

Sam cleared his throat, and for the first time since they met, he cracked a smile.

"I met him at a shopping mall signing autographs. He told me about the Odawa people being related to the Ojibwe and I think the Potawatomie as well. I didn't know a damn thing about Native Americans until I met Noc-a-Homa that day."

"I had a library card and began to read whatever I could find on Native Americans, from Iroquois Confederacy to The Trail of Tears, the Kiowa migrations, Apache Warriors, Peyote Ritual, all the dialects and creation myths."

Candy recognized a smell or sound she hadn't known in a long time, like sitting on a summer porch and hearing the soft purr of crickets in the surrounding darkness.

"I removed the photo from my bedroom wall," Sam explained to Candy, "and folded it carefully, like an American flag, tucked it in my back pack and just took off one day. I went west to Navajo country, over there in the four corners. There were a lot of cactus and canyons, wind and silence, dusty roads. I met a guy there who was a long distance runner, maybe in the army too. Anyway, he invited me over for cornbread at his Mom's and told me to come back when the sun came out the following spring."

It was 6 AM. Candy's shift was finished. Sam walked to the exit, and without looking behind him, held open the door for an extra few seconds. Candy and Sam walked together into a new morning.

The sun was spraying light everywhere, injecting life back into cars, buildings, and people. They reached the water tower on the eastern edge of North Avenue and sat down on the hill overlooking Lake Michigan.

"This is a great lake," said Sam, "as big as an ocean."

Candy agreed. "There's no way to see the other side and so many blues, so many blues I never knew before."

Candy lowered her head into Sam's lap and stretched out from head to toe. She rolled her ankles and wiggled her toes. She had a feeling Sam Doobins wanted to tell her everything and she was right.

# Ship Not Sinking

The sound of motorcades rustled families from indoor games onto porches, but there was no convoy, just a man with an exaggerated gait and straight back walking down the middle of the street. He barely touched the earth. There were no crusty sounds of boots crunching pebbles.

The more religiously bent wondered if this was the one, but there was no four-winged chariot. This was just a man and his brown river of Red Man juice gushing in spurts from a very human mouth.

When he reached the top of Danbury Hill, all lingering hopes deflated. The ordinary man scratched his crotch. The sight sobered some, grossed out others. But a few, mostly kids, nudged on by their fathers, inched closer to the man they had come to know in legends as Moonsher.

The children were scared and this caused fathers to cling, but fathers know archers let go of arrows so they moved out of the way and let their boys and girls make a human welcome tunnel. The children were in awe at Moonsher's size and wondered if it was true what their fathers had told them. Could he really throw The Pitch? Was this really Moonsher right there in front of them? Would he pass on the grip, delivery, and follow through?

Moonsher carried only a green gym bag with a fading St. Hedwig's Church insignia. He unpacked items nice and slow, adding to the suspense. He hummed while spreading out his snake oil equivalents. There was a contagious rhythm in the way he moved.

First came a tattered silver cloth that rolled 60 feet, six inches. Then a soap dish made of plastic, but shining like metal. This was followed by a fielder's mitt, a catcher's mitt, and finally, what looked like a cheese cloth bag filled with apples. The crowd wondered how so much could fit in such a small bag. Parents pointed to far away train tracks and overhead clouds and began seeing things that weren't really there.

Moonsher walked each item one at a time towards the pitcher's mound, pausing in between fair and foul territory to perform a detailed tapping ritual with his hands and feet. And when all the items had been arranged neatly beside the mound, he reached into the cheese cloth bag and grabbed not apples, but a baseball. He climbed up onto the mound and with his back perfectly straight, straddled the rubber. He then looked to home plate and shook off a few imaginary signs from an imaginary catcher. He sighed one last time before swirling into motion. Kids recognized the wheelbarrow wind up and ballerina leg kick and everyone in the audience ooohhhed and aaahhhed. The Pitch had arrived. Moonsher dismounted from the mound and smiled. "Ladies and gentleman," he said, with the voice of a carnival barker. "Let your children come closer."

Moonsher showed over 100 kids how to throw The Pitch that day, with only one or two demonstrating the necessary degree of dexterity, but the failures made them even hungrier to get it right.

Moonsher picked up his green gym bag, rubbed the St. Hedwig insignia and stomped across the outfield in a zigzag manner, looking back over his shoulder every once in a while. He climbed the waist high outfield fence and slowly melted into one of the dirt bike trails beyond centerfield. These were the same trails that would one day welcome each and every child onto paths far away from baseball.

Both parents and children looked on, feeling naked and alone. The children were the first to get on with their lives and they did so with an urgency and almost obligation to perfect The Pitch.

Some kids learned what they thought was The Pitch only to find out that pitchers on other teams could throw even harder and make the ball jump and dive even more. Other kids succumbed to dark thoughts or a girl's curves and drifted away from baseball. But there were some who picked up bats and tried their luck on the other side, as hitters, determined to hit The Pitch they never learned how to throw.

Benny Sands was one of them and he was the greatest hitter I ever saw. He batted left-handed and crouched as low as Cecil Cooper. I was certain Sands was a major leaguer in the making. Sands and another player on our high school team, Scott Milkins, asked me to be their batting practice pitcher because I threw strikes with no mustard.

It was at Land's End Park where we bumped into Moonsher. We didn't recognize him, but he remembered us—hard to believe since it was over 10 years ago—but there was no mistaking the sound of our names.

Moonsher carried the same St. Hedwig's bag, but looked skinnier and a lot shorter. He didn't stand up straight anymore. He slouched, but spoke in the same calm manner accentuating certain words.

"What d'ya say I stand out on the mound and throw you some?" His voice set free the memory in Sands and Milkins. They were reminded of failure, of never learning how to throw The Pitch. Their arrogant struts turned stiff. Sands began to adjust his belt. Milkins picked at his finger nails.

We let Moonsher throw a few pitches and he didn't disappoint. He couldn't have been throwing faster than 75 mph, but the ball moved. I served as the sit-in catcher. He hit my target right on the corner every pitch. Sands just stood there, refusing to grab a bat, so Moonsher stepped off the mound and walked towards home plate.

"Give me the bat then," he insisted. Sands resisted at first. He was scared. The risk was too high. If Moonsher could hit as well as he could pitch, Sands would have nothing. But he had no choice. Milkins and I wanted this to happen. It was two against one. I took the ball and was ready to pitch. Sands handed Moonsher the bat and shot me a glance from the corner of his eye as if to say, "put some oooomph into it."

I walked up on the mound and began to throw strikes like I was supposed to. Moonsher hit a few line drives, but mostly easy ground balls. He blamed it on his forearms, "too much like twigs," he said with a smile. "Maybe if I stand up straighter, lower my hands a bit, I'd feel loose as a goose like Eric Davis." Moonsher stepped away from the plate and repeated the name of the two-time all-star: "Eric Keith Davis." He spoke it in a slow, drawn out way, loud enough for everyone to hear, and then impersonated his swing.

Sands had been saved from shame. He perked up and became playful, impersonated Eric Davis too.

"I never got tired of watching him swagger to the plate," he said, "So easygoing like he was grabbing a beer from the fridge, looked like he could kill the ball or lay down an 8 ball corner pocket bunt single, and that's exactly what he did."

Sands hit four consecutive home runs that day. He repeated the same swing every time, smooth and easy, went with the pitch, hit to all fields and over all fences. I enjoyed pitching to him. He moved just like I envisioned a baseball player should move–mildly pigeon-toed, knees bent, hand in back pocket, slow and steady, spit. But Sands never did risk it all. He never dug in at the plate and faced Moonsher on the mound. It was his choice.

I combed the internet a few years ago in search of Sands' name, but only found lawyers, a few real estate agents, and a couple dozen Facebook pages. I checked baseball-reference.com and thebaseballcube.com for Sands sightings on Independent League rosters, but there was nothing.

It wasn't the first time my pseudo bird dog scout visions came up as duds and it wouldn't be the last, but I was in good company. Sparky Anderson once declared Chris Pitarro the next Brooks Robinson.

Benny Sands had the swing of Ken Griffey Jr., Ted Williams, and Mickey Mantle. I knew it wouldn't be easy for him. I knew that apples didn't magically appear at grocery stores stacked in a pyramid shape. I knew it took two years or maybe ten for the seed to bloom into a tree and then another couple of months for the apple to ripen followed by more time and effort to be picked and packed, trucked, delivered, and displayed in that aisle seven pyramid of Macintosh, Red Delicious, Spartan, or Granny Smiths. There were no guarantees. They could bruise and brown and fall to the fertilizer floor with the rest of us nobodies.

Ted Williams was a mad scientist studying every last detail of his own swing and the opposing pitchers' motion. Griffey Jr. read his destiny clearly. Mantle apparently stumbled 12-pack drunk to the plate and smacked a 480 foot homer and then for good measure hit a second long ball from the other side. But none of them relied on magic. In their own way, it was all about sweat and toil, a little bit of luck and taking risks.

Wherever Benny Sands is, I hope he hears the life lesson I've come to understand, *"What you do may seem useless, but do it anyway."* I hope he hears it every damn waking day. But Benny Sands, I fear, does not hear this. He stands at a bar rail instead and speaks in could ofs and should ofs and what ifs.

I haven't seen Sands or Moonsher in over 10 years, but I'm reminded of both in the strangers I meet at bar rails, in bus cabins, or anywhere conversation sparks up. I hear two distinct voices, sometimes in two different people and sometimes at war within myself. It's the Benny Sands voice of regret and the Moonsher that still dreams.

I sit in my TV room and watch the Milwaukee Brewers' Jean Segura backhand a sharp grounder deep in the hole, his feet touching the outfield grass. He bows on one leg and from a squatting position throws an off balance 98-mph strike to Mark Reynolds at first base. Segura is 24 years young and moves so effortlessly, like he's in a dream and free from the worldly constraints of ribs and joints and gravity.

It's easy to imagine him flashing that same grace 100 years ago. I wonder if the awe and excitement I feel is the same my grandfather enjoyed while watching the great players up close and in person, before there even was TV.

I think grandpa needed baseball the same way I do—the Moonsher way. Grandpa spoke with the same enthusiasm about Ted Williams as he did Ken Griffey Jr. He called both their swings "slow and easy, almost perfect."

Grandpa watched the Dead Ball Era give way to a live one. He watched neighborhoods and stadiums get destroyed. He experienced ugly financial realities, AstroTurf, domes, free agency. And none of that cooled his passion. He loved the game on the diamond where it hadn't really changed. Yes, the mounds were lowered in 1969. The American League-only DH was added in 1973. The spit ball was supposedly banned, and so on.

But the bases were still 90 feet apart. There were still three outs to an inning, four balls for a walk, batters hitting behind runners, pitchers working out of jams, and late inning home runs.

Even before my grandpa and before Babe Ruth and Ty Cobb, in the days of Cap Anson and King Kelly, the Philadelphia Quakers and Cleveland Spiders, nine balls for a walk, then eight, six, five, and finally four in 1879, pitchers throwing underhand or sidearm until 1884 when the modern overhand motion was no longer banned.

Even then, it must have been wasting away entire days at ballparks and talk of the game leaking into churches and bars, sandlots, bed at night with the lights off and still wanting more.

It's late now. I can see the moon. My own son squirms in his seat, rubs his eyes. He's tired, but determined to stretch the day as long as possible. He asks to hear the same story he's heard dozens of times before. We walk side by side to his bedroom without saying a word. He tucks his feet under the covers and waits for me to begin.

*The sound of motorcades rustled families from indoor games onto porches, but there was no convoy, just a man with an exaggerated gait and straight back walking down the middle of the street. He barely touched the earth. There were no crusty sounds of boots crunching pebbles...*

# Never Wears a Watch

I crease the corners of books with triangles like a squirrel gathers and stashes nuts so I have somewhere to turn on a dull day like pages 118-119 of *Baseball in America* by Robert Smith. The book is an excellent coffee table history, pictures galore including Terra-cotta figures from the Toltec period, primitive religious rites, or as the caption wonders, inventors of baseball? There are fans in suits and ties and derby hats, Nick Altrock dodging 1906 White Sox crowds, Jim Thorpe, and on and on go the early years of baseball.

There's a photo of Myrtle Rowe and another of her team. She's surrounded by baseball boys. The pictures don't correspond to the narrative. Three Fingered Mordecai Brown is discussed to the right of Myrtle Rowe's photographs. So is Toad Ramsey's bent index finger and "Joseph Wood, a demon pool player called Smoky Joe because of the imaginary smoke his fast ball emitted."

There's one simple sentence to finish off page 119 and it sends me upriver back to Myrtle's cheeks and determined straight jaw and all it says is,

"Eddie Plank, a left-handed Pennsylvania farm boy who had gone to college late (graduated at twenty-five) and discovered while he was there that his practice of knocking birds off fences with stones had given the strength and cunning to his arm that made a baseball pitcher great."

One of these years I'll reach chapter 10 of that book and the double page photo sequence of Herb Score's pitching motion. The next page is the same Score, but he's looking more like an Egyptian mummy, ace bandages wrapped around his forehead and left eye. He's just been hit by a Gil McDougald line drive.

Here today and gone tomorrow and revived on some strange face in some unexpected place and time and holy crap, it's Eri Yoshida, the knuckleball princess. Is that even possible?

Dear Eri,

*I should have written earlier, maybe when you first met Tim Wakefield and dreamed of being a big league pitcher. God, it's hard enough to make it past the airport security of destiny's drunk chariot driver, a wrong last name and what not, let alone being a knuckleballer and a Japanese teenage girl to boot.*

*I won't even pretend to know what kind of roles and duties and responsibilities are expected of you, the tradition tradition tradition, but I can tell you this, sweet knuckleball princess. You came to a baseball land where crotch scratching, American Flags, and spitting is grace and you still fly.*

*You're like a Japanese Harry Houdini performing miracles in an unexpected hurricane realizing democracy's dream day after day after day!*

*Houdini knew the rules, knew the game, the world, chained and bound, volumes of water pressure pushing him down further and still sinking to his eventual battle field, a ring of toil and strain. He accepted the conditions and added a few more chains around his knees and neck, handcuffs and just to be certain there was no way out, blindfolded!*

*And as the crowd waited lustily to be wowed and entertained, Houdini took a deep inhale and exhale and inhale and exhale and then slowly performed amazing, magical, continuous, one after another acts of escape, of the people, for the people, so help him god, exhale, bravo, encore.*

*Caste systems, as subtle as they may be in today's world are barely static on your radar Eri and I have a crush on your will and smell you in evergreen tree branches that refuse to fall in winter.*

*I read that you're trying out for the Hyogo Blue Sandars, a Japanese Indy team. You're like a geriatric's last breath, but still determined to crank out one last Phil Niekro. I feel 20 years young again.*

*Take care,*
*your fan forever*

*

The odds of a messiah arriving always seem about the same as a geisha, in Montreal anyway, but the odds spike a bit when entering a stadium, even if it's only Éloi Viau Stadium, home of the LaSalle Cardinals of the LBEQ, Ligue de Baseball Elite Quebec, highest amateur level in the province.

There are no giant cement sidewalk ramps twirling around the stadium periphery, no fans running free and easy, smashing every empty beer cup in sight, their own gong show symphony.

No, there's none of that but it is 323 feet down both lines and the pitcher's mound always looks like a burial mound because someone pitched before and the PA announcer says things like, "Now pitching for LaSalle, #34 Jon Paul Castigneau" and the outfield grass is very green and the third baseman with hand in back pocket spits sunflower seeds. There are maybe 40 people at the game and they're scrunched into seats on the third base side. Most are family members or a player's love interest.

The outfield alleys look like an abandoned red light district, all empty and dark, nothing but bumps and dead ends. That's when Myrtle Rowe and Eri Yoshida and that demon pool player Smoky Joe come tumbling through time, defying gravity and all the other rules.

Myrtle plays all kinds of positions including catcher and she never flinches or turns her shoulders when the batter swings. She can hop over tree rings and is willing to unfasten the shin guards she doesn't own anyway and fling them out of this decade and century like a stripper letting go the pole, racing towards the mound to impersonate Sandy Koufax's round house wind up.

She's not the least bit burdened by pride or genocide and quickly switches to the samurai slicing of Rod Carew and then right back to the mound doing her Neshek therapy—a spastic pre-pitch ritual, a woman playing twister with 7 ghosts.

She relates to pine tar and a flag pole with the same passion as she does her grandma's home-stitched quilt. She accepts all monikers, nicknames, and handles them with the same grace.

*"Ladies and Gentleman, Boys and Girls, Meet the one and only Myrtle "The Murderer's" Rowe."*

She sings too and wears all the dances of the world in her eyes. One minute she's hopping a train-out-of-town and the next minute she holds an entire bar room hostage with kindness, all her river cook up barbecue stories with those old Indian names like Leaning Cedar.

She's a gambler and loves to loosen ties, a perfect trade deadline addition to any team in any league, from Peace River, Alberta to Las Mochis, Mexico and anywhere in between.

Maybe she never had a mother or father, never a country, sport, or song either, one day is red bangs cut straight like a Geisha and tomorrow it's lipstick and an erotic San Bernardino whine, an ideal utility player.

Some called her slut, bitch, thespian, or even worse—designated hitter—pacing between a clubhouse video room and the water cooler dugout. She rises up anyway, always one eye on the pitcher like a roof top sniper. Most people are scared so they pretend she's not real, but she hits the ball without the luxury of amnesia, that playing defense on grass between at bats, to free her mind from the burden of seven consecutive deadly trips to the plate and how many runners left on base?

She rides opening day's electricity all the way to Game 7, brings clean up hitters to their knees. The ball boys eye her up and down as she walks through the clubhouse tunnel and whispers, "never more than this moment," and yet she's not vain. She would never hook a man, woman, or even a journalist and then set them free in a cloud of her own exhaust blowing their lonely harmonicas in strained worship.

She's all about doubleheaders and extra innings, coming to life when the bar lights are on and when the tender says, "Time to go home folks." She gives you a tap dance, a pluck on a sea lion's whisker, a made up Mezuzah of words....

*"I'm a date palm,"*
*exactly like it says in the Bible.*

*"I'm Katie Casey"*
*exactly like it says in the song*
*and when they ask her about geishas*
*she says,*

*"I'm a peacock,"*
*as she slips back into the outfield alley darkness.*

*

I've only seen Mr. Jack Chesbro on a picture, not from that book *[Baseball in America.]* It's a different book. I can't remember the title, but there are many photos of Sweet Caporal Tobacco baseball cards and one of them is Chesbro and I wonder if he experienced the same sensation standing there on the mound, daydreaming of stepping outside the chalk lines, to escape whatever monotony may have gripped him?

I doubt it. Jack Chesbro never creased the pages of books for a dull day or I won't let myself believe he did and I'm not budging on this because he threw 260 complete games in 11 years and how many thousands of pitches? Over and over the celluloid rolls, forever trapped in the leading role, the workhorse of 12-hour shifts.

Complete games barely exist anymore and no one shovels cow manure in the off-season to supplement their income, but Jack Chesbro is more than a memory. Kids in Tuscaloosa,

Boise, Sudbury, or Kyoto dream behind the internet café and play Christy Mathewson, tossing black and white baseballs at an 8-pane window with spit-change-ups so sublime, they stop in mid-flight, perfectly located…

8 pitches…

8 panes…

8 strikes…

and not one broken glass
because once upon a time there was no forkball either.


Quotes in this story come from the book *Baseball in America* by Robert Smith; Holt, Rinehart and Winston, New York, 1961.

# Running from the Shackles

Even test tubes collect dust. All breakthrough gadgets enjoy a "gotta have it" craze. The once prized luxury items then transform into necessity followed by mass production and junkyard bouquet, dust.

"And that's alright," says little Hupskin Harold "Because the days of slim pickings are no fun at all." Harold was the son of a farmer, worked sunrise to sundown and one day, when daddy was cleaning out the pig pen, Harold ventured where daddy always said, "Off Limits." That's where he stumbled on a crate filled with beakers and he just had to know so he opened the crate and one beaker was labeled *Rarámuri* and another, *Lumberjack*.

Harold knew plenty about lumberjacks. His father came from a long line of loggers from the Pacific Northwest. He was the first Hupskin to break free from the Lumberjack mold. He longed to try something new and pursued vegetable farming instead.

Harold knew a lot less about the *Rarámuri*, only that they spoke an Uto-Aztecan language and that the Spanish didn't call them *Rarámuri*. They referred to them as "Tarahumara."

Harold's social studies teacher who the kids called Joe was a descendant of the *Rarámuri* and that's how Harold came to know about them.

And so it felt like more than a coincidence when he discovered a test tube with *Rarámuri* written on it. Harold felt an excitement like never before. He took a third beaker, an empty one, and mixed the two liquids of Lumberjack and Tarahumara together. There were burps and bubbles and all kinds of smoke billows. Hupskin Harold never told a soul. He hid the new beaker behind the horse stable, far away from the pig pen and daddy. and then he slipped it gently inside an old Burtz Beer crate and covered it with willow and bamboo branches.

Hupskin Harold rode his daddy's tractor bumpity-bump over the abandoned field right to the very spot of the beakers. And that's where he transplanted the test tube embryo from genie bottle beaker to aquarium and then to a human port-a-potty where it soon became a fetus and grew even bigger. The *Rarámuri*/Lumberjack became so big that Harold had no choice but to let him loose early spring one year. It was the darnedest thing the way that hybrid boy leaped and sprinted nowhere in particular. He was as healthy as can be, no different from a child born from the birds and bees.

The *Rarámuri* were no secret to big league baseball, nestled in the Copper Canyon-Mexican state of Chihuahua. There was no game to hunt or weeds to chew there, so natives ran up and down the canyon in search of protein and built up plenty of endurance in the process, capable of running 50 miles in a single day. Their efforts made a grueling 162 game baseball grind seem like a paddle boat ride across a still lake.

Big league reps sent their best wordsmiths to seduce the *Rarámuri* into setting free one of their young boys in the hopes of landing baseball gold. The reps winked their eyes and promised millions of dollars in return, but the "pillars of the sky," as the *Rarámuri* called themselves, had no use for money. They were a chosen people and not interested in mixing with "sons of the devil."

Harold asked his teacher Joe all sorts of questions about the *Rarámuri*. "Does the word race originate with them? It would make sense since they're so fast and can run so far." Joe put his arm around young Hupskin. "And they seem like such a proud and confident people," Harold continued. "I wonder if they burn everything they touch to prevent cloning." Joe laughed and so did Harold, but he was sort of serious too.

It seems strange that Hupskin Harold's father, way up north in Idaho, would find a stray strand from a *Rarámuri* cloak, but "life ain't nothing but a dream" said Harold's momma—Miss Margaret.

Daddy took a close look at the strand and in the company of his son, shrugged it off as tumbleweed, but in the secret hours of the night he set to work in his makeshift lab, whipping up separate test tube brews of *Rarámuri* and Lumberjack. Hupskin Harold and his boyhood curiosity took care of the rest, mixing the dexterity and power of a Lumberjack with the speed and smarts of *Rarámuri*. Harold never did have a pet.

The hybrid boy had the mind of a new-born, couldn't read a stop sign, suffered from bed wetting too, but boy-oh-boy could he run with a smile. And when the time was right and the boy just ripe, Harold taught him how to throw and hit a baseball.

Hupskin Harold's father spotted the hybrid as summer lost its heat and he knew immediately what his son had done, but didn't say a thing, not until the colors of the grass changed into harvest hues of light brown and yellow and the sky became a purple bruise and the world a great big ball of ochre.

Only then did he suggest father and son take a walk. The two waltzed among tall yellow grasses and neither one of them said a word. They enjoyed the swishing sound dry grass made against their denim blue jeans. And for Harold, it probably meant the postponement of his punishment. But Daddy was a vegetable farmer and he expected the unexpected in both the skies above and the land he tilled. And so he embraced his son's experiment, referred to it as "fruits of my son's curiosity" and called him "a chip off the old block."

And so they worked together, gave their test tube a name—Tunis—and raised him up, and Idaho baseball was never quite the same. Tunis hit balls from foul line to foul line and everywhere in between, turned a spray chart of base hits into a Jackson Pollock painting. He could pitch too, struck out everything in sight. But it was the way he held the bat like a samurai sword that wowed everyone and the way he took a running start in the batter's box and lifted that leg so high and what a strange swing like he was chopping wood, sky to earth, and yet he hit the ball wherever he willed it to go. Heads spun around 360 degrees. Jaws dropped. This was an 8th wonder of the world situation.

And when Tunis came of baseball age—10 years young—the big league scouts and tycoons arrived, loaded with promises and offer sheets, brandishing their best woo and persuasion.

Daddy and Hupskin Harold tossed all their bids in a straw hat and requested a fortnight to think it over.

Then Tunis, Harold, and daddy all went for dinner at daddy's shotgun shack and no one knows for sure what happened. Miss Margaret whipped up her wheat grass and pork rind soup. The Hassey girls practiced their kicks. The three men fell asleep beside Burtz bottles. Fourteen days and nights passed, one Burtz beer after another, but the 15th day was different. They smoked pipes and guzzled three cups of sassafras tea instead and were overcome by wanderlust. They raced outside and into the truck, headed south. They drove all the way till morning and never stopped.

The scouts and tycoons were in the hundreds by then, their unsigned contracts waving in the wind and their faces drooping with sorrow. They looked east and west, north, and south. They looked up and down and everywhere, but there was no sign of Tunis, only trains fading away just as fast as they had come in. Hupskin Harold and his father were gone and they had brought their prized test tube Tunis with them.

The tycoons hopped on the next breeze out-of-town, following the trail of Tunis. Miss Margaret stood on the porch and watched. "Just chasing their tails. Ain't no one ever caught Hupskin and his father," she whispered, suddenly in need of warmth and comfort. But before the trail of tycoon exhaust had vanished, a new posse of men filled the glade. They were louder and smelled funkier and most of them were in desperate need of a dentist. In fact, some had no teeth at all.

Old Man Miggins was the first to step forward. He grabbed the closest crate he could find, mounted the rickety box, and began to speak. "Ain't none of us seen a player who hits the ball like Tunis, runs or fields like him, ain't that right boys?" The question needed no answer. Old Man Miggins continued.

"Comb every last corner of Miss Margaret's ranch and find whatever secret that old man and his son are hiding." Miggins removed his straw hat and shook his head in disbelief. "Ain't no one who hits a baseball like that Tunis. No one ever has and no one ever will, not Joe Jackson, not Ted Williams, not Tony Gwynn, and we're gonna find out how and why and whatever it is, we're gonna get it and whip us up a batch of ball players, our own ball players."

"We'll make 'em more than five tool players," shouted Andrew Tinsel.

"Fans will flock to our stadiums," chimed in Piper Durbins.

Old Man Miggins stepped down from the crate and made his way into the large circle that had formed. He moved to the center and began again. "We'll run those big league bosses out of business."

There were a dozen tycoons in the Miggins posse and all of 'em let out a wild west YAHOOOOOO. None of them was ever affiliated with baseball, nothing organized anyway. Some of them played in whiskey and beer leagues and a few others waxed on and on about their Russian relatives making the trek south, from Siberia across the Bering Strait to Alaska, Yukon, and Northern California to where the Russian river still flows.

"Barnstorming by canoe," they explained. "Trading furs when everyone else was panning for gold, our grandpas raised all kinds of hell playing that old, Russian game of Lapta up and down the river. Musta been one long hootenanny with all that gambling, cheating, and stealing."

The other tycoons let out another wild west YAHOOOOOO. They were a hoodlum mix of car thieves, con artists, and drug dealers—some  sketchy with pock marks on their foreheads or scars under their eyes, and others looking fresh as a baby's ass and smelling mint green too. Some wore cowboy boots with sharp spurs and others soft slip-on loafers, but they all shared the same lifelong fascination—to knock the biggest bosses off their thrones. It didn't matter what racket they were in—steel mills, coal mines, silicon, or gold. As long as bosses were big, they were good game to hunt, topple and kick to the ground, and kick dirt on their graves for good measure.

Some of the men Miggins recruited. Others, like Kid Creedle, simply followed their noses and found their way. If plants turn towards the sun, then Kid Creedle and all members of the Miggins minyan turned the opposite way—towards  the darkest clouds to ever roam a summer sky.

Kid Creedle never met a bottle of bourbon he didn't adore. The time of day or season didn't matter. He was always sipping from his silver hip flask and was always happy. He wore a suit coat with a fresh flower pinned to his lapel and was as calm as can be. It was hard to tell if he was on his way to church or getting ready to pass out. The uncertainty made him one hell of a poker player too.

"Wino Luxury Boxes," Kid Creedle suggested. "We'll send hound dogs to sniff out hobos fuming a vagabond stench."

"That glorious mix of mother earth, iron, and body odor," added Miggins.

"We'll escort them into liquor-furnished corporate boxes, all across baseball, and let 'em drink and rant and rave." Kid Creedle took a bow and everyone let out a good long laugh.

"We'll expand the operation," said Miggins, "Into wino Olympics with shopping kart races around the base paths."

"And two-sided sandwich boards between innings," added Mr. Tinsel. "The prettiest dames we can find, flashing their peacock plumage around the bases. Lot lizards running free on the diamond. We'll fill up stadiums from Boise to Timbuktu."

"Hold your horses," warned Old Man Miggins. "There ain't no baseball in Egypt, not yet anyway, but only because we haven't been there." And that was followed by another collective Wild West YAHOOOOOO and a round of gut-wrenching laughter. All came to a sudden stop with the sound of a colt .45 exploding in the virgin air. It was Miggins way of saying, "time to get down to dirty business."

"I reckon this Hupskin Harold and his father made damn sure all traces of beakers and mad science were removed before they vanished," said Miggins. "But they ain't jewel thieves like some of us. They shoved off in a big old tornado haste of a hurry. They musta left a track or two somewhere."

Miggins waved his open hands towards himself, a signal for everyone to gather round like a meeting on the pitcher's mound. In a soft whisper, he said, "Or maybe it's just a hair follicle, but I reckon whatever it is will lead us straight to the prize."

Andrew Tinsel found a test tube just before sundown and waved it high in the air. Another round of "YAHOOOOO's" followed. Poor Miss Margaret scrunched her nose and squinted her eyes in confusion. She had no idea what all the fuss was about. She had found the beaker many moons ago and put it to good use, as a mixing bowl for her world-famous Baraboo blueberry pie.

But no one bothered explaining a darn thing to her and so the Hupskin farm cleared out faster than a honky-tonk during a police raid. The boys drove far away to where no one knew a damn thing about Tunis. Miggins sent the test tube to a big city lab and it didn't take more than a day or two for the DNA results to arrive.

Microscopic details clearly described 2.8 parts *Rarámuri* to 1.9 parts Lumberjack. And under the print out was a shiny brochure, promising "the most perfect baseball body types." There were 11 pages in all, with step-by-step manuals listing the required tools, proper incubation temperatures, and all the necessary ingredients to create a 25-man roster of ideal prototypes, of pitchers provoking never-before-seen whiff rates and batters fouling off pitches into 3 AM rainy nights, defenders crawling walls and making throws with dartboard accuracy.

Ethnic and personality traits could be manufactured with a little mixing of some prefabricated stew. Hair or eye color, height, width, temperament, and IQ required nothing but a few sprinkles of special spice packs. Miggins raised a glass and said, "All that's fine and dandy, but there's one crucial ingredient missing." And before anyone's wonder slipped into worry, Miggins raised up his closed fist—a beacon of darkness—and yelled, "We are the missing ingredient, boys. We are the wicked men destined to carry out this evil plan! We will make the greatest baseball players the world has ever known."

"The strongest and most beautiful," added Kid Creedle.

"Most flexible and mean," said Piper Durbins.

The Miggins minyan hired the best and brightest minds in the world, from gene experts to biomedical engineers to statistical baseball whizzes and together they designed hundreds of baseball prototypes, in order to form a more perfect baseball species.

"A catcher needs the genes of a plumber," said Piper Durbins. "All that squatting and reaching and handling of tools is perfectly suited for a man behind the plate."

"And a steady diet of hot dogs and pig's feet too," added Kid Creedle. "The extra cushion of fat will protect him from foul tips."

"A first baseman needs the gracious hospitality of a Bedouin tent dweller," chimed in Old Man Miggins.

"To seduce with friendly talk," added Piper Durbins. "So when the runner/guest least expects it, he gets nabbed by a well-timed pick-off play."

Families were chosen throughout the world to nurture and raise up the test tube hybrids, and in some cases tri-breeds, into fully functioning human being baseball players. Devices were implanted into each baby's right shin. The minuscule metal box had a built-in homing device linking test tubes to their masters.

A giant train station scoreboard was rigged up to monitor their progress, as each member evolved from slide show specimen to fetus, then toddler and boy and finally baseball player. The league was to be called Free from Genetic Restriction, or FFGR, but the acronym didn't spell a damn thing so it was changed to League of Free, or LOF.

The 100-year old Big League Circuit or BLC enjoyed a monopoly over all of professional baseball and they weren't the least bit worried by the emergence of the LOF. And why would they be? There were no threats to their dominion, no stand-out players or teams in the LOF, and as a result, no devoted fans kangaroo-ing over to the LOF side, not yet anyway. The hybrids were years away from strutting their stuff across big league diamonds, but those years passed quickly, kind of snuck up on BLC bosses. Paranoia and suspicion soon filled their minds.

Old Man Miggins anticipated this would happen and so he arranged for undercover marketing masters to infiltrate BLC ranks. They explained to BLC bosses how competition from the new LOF would spike the BLC profits beyond previous highs.

"You have to believe," the *marketeers* encouraged. "All will be better," they promised. "You may think the BLC is great and powerful today, but just you wait. It will soon thrive like never before and make baseball fans the happiest lot in the universe!"

The plan worked wonders. BLC pride had been tickled. Suspicions mellowed. Order and calm was restored.

Herschel Shmenkins was the first player to cause a stir in BLC minds. He was 2.8 parts Orthodox Jew and 2.4 parts Inuit Eskimo and smuggled into a Teklavitch Hasidic community. He awoke every morning and washed his hands, said a ritual prayer, walked to the synagogue, wrapped leather straps and parchment-filled prayer boxes around his head and arm. He prayed three times a day and before bed too, six days a week with a 7th inning stretch or Shabbat-day-of-rest, to round out the weekly ritual.

Herschel cultivated incredible discipline and precision performing his prayers Monday to Sunday, 365 days a years, so when it came time to pitch, he was quite adept at repeating the same motion, syncing hips, arms and legs, the same slot and follow through...mind, body, and soul, paint the corner, strike three so help him God.

The Inuit side of Herschel's hybrid provided a whale hunter's endurance, and what ingenuity in carving igloo windows from blocks of ice! A single blade of grass coupled with sunshine could then spark a fire, even in the dead of winter. Herschel, as a result, possessed incredible eye-hand coordination and patience. The long days his ancestors spent tracking an animal required a knowledge of the land, to better recognize the tracks and trails of animals, the flow of a river, types of trees. This translated well into baseball pitcher speak because Herschel remembered every nuance of every hitter. There was no talk of relief pitchers when he took the mound.

Players were spread out team-to-team in the larger LOF League and players of all ages and skill levels were welcome. When you have a pitcher like Herschel Shmenkins striking out 16, 17, and 14 batters over three consecutive starts, a team can survive with a right fielder sprawled out on a lawn chair spitting sunflower seeds.

Herschel gave up a mere two infield hits over that three game stretch so the crowd baited him to "do a Satchel" as in Satchel Paige, and "motion your defense to take a seat," but Herschel knew what lurked around the corner, none other than right fielder Javier "Downtown" Torres Iglesias.

Javier hit a home run every nine at-bats, almost two fewer trips to the plate than Babe Ruth, and Iglesias launched shooting stars of at least 500 feet. This was the same Iglesias who could drop down a bunt and run 90 feet in 3.2 seconds, the same

Iglesias possessing shot put power for an outfield arm and an archer's accuracy. Five tools? More like an entire tool chest!! Iglesias was a tri-breed mix of an Ethiopian King, delicate jewel thief, and anthropology professor. He was raised in Odessa, Texas.

Stadiums were small in the LOF with maximum seating capacity 7,500. This was designed to inspire the want but can't have in a fan's heart, draw them closer to the radio and groove of Leifman Sprout's voice.

Leifman weaved play-by-play action with colorful biography, making a delicious tapestry for the ear. He turned players into legends, but only after making a quick pick in the hole or hitting a ground ball to advance a runner. He didn't bother with predictions or expertise. The transcripts and recordings of Leifman broadcasts were traded on street corners the following day.

> *"Ralph Dertwood would have made one hell of a sea captain, never met a gale wind he couldn't tame, and who needs a glove at the hot corner anyway? Dertwood snared fish with his bare hands growing up along the Cumberland River."*

Leifman told no lies. Dertwood did grow up along the Cumberland River, in Eastern Tennessee, as a member of the Melungeon Tribe—a unique triracial mix of African, European, and Native American ancestry, an isolated mountain dwelling people surviving on subsistence farming.

> *"Ralph stands in now to face a pitcher who also hails from Tennessee, Mr. Darrin Dreelskins, and look at that, Dertwood lays a bunt down the third base line,*

*so perfectly placed it would take curling sweepers to repeat the same trajectory and balance, the ball somehow not rolling foul. Nothing the defense can do but watch in disbelief as the ball hugs the line, and that's just what they do. Dertwood sure keeps us guessing: One at bat it's a 365-foot missile off the wall and now a well-placed bloop single over the first baseman's head, but always the same result. Dertwood reaches base safely."*

Tickets to games were as rare as blue moons, but no one complained. They either tuned to Leifman or looked up at giant street billboards modeled after the ones 100 years ago, the ones looking like pinball machines with lights and numbers to indicate runners on base, how many outs, the names and number of fielders, who was at bat, who was on deck, who was on the mound, who was warming up in the bullpen, and runs, hits, and errors.

Thousands of fans gathered in downtown streets where pamphlets were distributed with updates on games and related LOF events as well. Fans not the least bit interested in baseball were drawn to the words of Ian Meshowitz and his Daily Decree as his column came to be called.

## The Daily Decree

### There's Still .338

by Ian Meshowitz

*We long for days of baseball records untouchable, back when we stared at lists of those with 3,000 hits, and whenever the name Cobb was spoken, it felt like an old secret exposed; "Thou shalt never take Cobb's name in vain."*

*Players existed in a black and white baseball world where time and death didn't exist and maybe the players didn't either. George Herman Ruth, Tyrus Raymond Cobb, and Rogers Hornsby were perfect and no one was named Tyrus, not on today's streets anyway.*

*And yet, every once in a while, someone jackhammers those names and sacred numbers and our brick wall of tradition shatters within us. There's an opening into that invincible other dimension and the unreachable becomes oh so real, because Pete Rose cracked 3,000 hits and the dam walls dynamite and a flood flows with Lou Brock, Carl Yastrzemski, Rod Carew, Robin Yount, George Brett, and so on and so forth. And now Gregory Sanara is upon us. He, too, has penetrated that veil.*

*The playboy turned ballplayer says he "adores being with the people" as much as he does flashing leather. He's a ballet dancer, tip toe artist, and that's only half the story. He hits baseballs, or excuse me, he guides 'em like drone missiles.*

*Sanara grew up walking fashion runways, modeling diapers, toy trains, and finally designer jeans. It was on board those very runways where he developed that one-of-a-kind strut we've been forced to get used to this inaugural season because of his 30 home runs. Mom and dad sent him to Paris, Milan, New York City, and maybe most memorable of all, Tokyo, Japan, where Sanara said, "I want more hits than anyone in the world."*

*The words spoken at a time when Sanara didn't even play baseball. The leap he's made since then is not measurable in human terms, not after eclipsing George Sisler's 257 hits in a single season and just last night, topping Ichiro's 262 to become all time king. And yet no one is even certain what Sanara meant by "I want more hits than anyone."*

*Was it Shing Pang Fu hits, as in full contact blows, or musical hits? Sanara also plays the piano and is a black belt so we may never know for sure, but let's be grateful baseball fans that Sanara expressed a desire to play. Praises to his parents who bought him more than a custom-made Soturo infielder's glove. They invested in a pitching machine and hired chefs, plumbers, infielders, and hitters to train their child and acquire all the skills and dexterity required to be the best shortstop in the world and well, seven years later, we never see the same Sanara two days in a row and yesterday was no different.*

*With the score tied 2-2, bottom of the ninth, Sanara swung at a 3-0 pitch two feet above his head. He raised those soft, silky hands and chopped down with a vicious thrust with what is now well-known as Sanara's Shing Pang Fu Chop. Sanara was standing on first base by the time the spheroid returned to earth. He then proceeded to steal second and third and score the winning run on a sacrifice fly.*

One Daily Decree after another, yet even Ian Meshowitz would never know that Gregory Sanara was a hybrid mix of a European King and a Brazilian Capoeira martial art dancer, or that Sanara was the living test tube embodiment of Tunis, "the one who got away."

There were only eight teams in that first year with two divisions—an East and a West, all within the same city limits and all reachable by public transportation. Fans began fleeing BLC stadiums and for what? To stand among masses of people in downtown streets and watch a pinball scoreboard light up? To hunch in bedroom corners and listen to Leifman Sprout babble on? To sit along the Shendike Lagoon and read Ian Meshowitz's Daily Decree dribble? The BLC were dumbfounded and took action.

They sent undercover spies into the LOF, to lure catcher Ivan Moop and doubles machine, Jack Skaggs, over to the BLC side in the hope of creating a trend. The homing devices, however, worked to robotic perfection. Whenever the Big League Circuit was mentioned, Moop and Skaggs suffered mild electrical shocks, more than enough to turn them against any attractive offers. The coup was thwarted.

BLC owners then proposed an all-star team of LOF players to compete against an all-star team of BLC players. It would be a month-long tour to entertain fans across the world. The BLC agreed to absorb all TV costs since the LOF had no TV. The LOF agreed to showcase its talent on a one month tour under one condition—the winners would absorb the losers and rule the baseball world. This would be an all or nothing competition. Winner takes all.

The brains behind the LOF were misfit gamblers who had been playing high stakes since the third grade. They had nothing to lose, while the more conservative BLC, well, they had no choice, financially speaking. Their own fans had already begun fleeing BLC stadiums, attracted to the more exciting LOF players.

The LOF won seven of the first eight games. Moop and Skaggs both caught fire. Meshowitz had a field day in his pamphlet, referring to the turn of events as payback for the BLC messing with LOF players.

> *"Ivan Moop looked more like a mime artist behind the plate, framing pitches and altering the minds of umpires, molding them at will like lumps of clay with balls becoming strikes. Offensively, Jack Skaggs enjoyed what appeared to be an extended batting practice, socking six home runs, four doubles, four singles, and walking 8 times for a batting average of .620. He drove in 21 runs and established a new LOF record with 44 total bases in one week's work."*

Meshowitz would never know that Moop was a hybrid of a Balkan Hora dancer and Australian dairy farmer. And he would never know that Skaggs was a tribreed mix of Israeli Kibbutz, Amazonian Shaman, and accordion mechanic.

The LOF won 10 of 13 games and heading into the 3rd week, needed only four wins to put a nail in the BLC coffin. The next four games, however, were to be played on the western fringes of the BLC, requiring the LOF to surrender their preferred and only method of travel—bus.

The DC 930 carrying LOF all-stars reached its cruising altitude of 35,000 feet. The drink cart was just beginning to make its way through the cabin when a sudden screeching sound was heard. The plane began to nosedive out of control, falling fast and furious, scraping through trees and crash, splat, somewhere near Black Hills, South Dakota. All the passengers died on impact.

The initial investigation unveiled bodies with exposed coils and charred wires, but this had nothing to do with the plane or its metal parts. The smoke and smell came from LOF players and their homing devices, still smouldering by the time aviation authorities arrived. The entire test tube conspiracy was soon exposed.

The LOF were charged with engineering the most perverse scandal to ever hit the cherished tradition of baseball, but there was more. The BLC were also accused of orchestrating the crash in order to kill off the competition.

The search for the evil posse of LOF owners unified the baseball nation with collective hate aimed at finding the "evil bastards" and bringing them to justice.

But the Miggins men were no strangers to a chase. They were already saddled and well into their giddy up, fleeing from justice before the first flames from the airplane fire had a chance to cool. By morning, local authorities aptly nicknamed them the "Terrible Twelve" — Wanted Dead or Alive.

It took three long weeks of combing forests and prairies, but all members of the Miggins minyan were caught and brought to trial except Old Man Miggins. He remained on the loose. A hungry hunt ensued, but as time wore on, tempers mellowed and Miggins became more folk hero than villain. Candle vigils were held, songs sung.

Miggins had slipped into a monk's robe the moment he had heard of the crash. He packed a bag, walked to the bus station, and headed south towards the same destination he'd been so many times before—no man's land—to  start over, this time as a drunk hobo monk.

Miggins walked and walked and finally descended into a dusty valley where he recognized the surround sound of an Indian tongue. He reached into his saddle bag and pulled out the bottle of Irish Rose rot gut wine he had opened the night before. Miggins soon spotted a trio under a tree. One of them was running in place.

Miggins moved closer and knew right away. It was Hupskin Harold and his father. Hupskin had the beginnings of a beard and dad slouched a bit, but other than that, they both looked about the same. And Tunis was as fresh and springy as ever.

Miggins didn't bother being discreet. He didn't have to be. Tunis had never met Old Man Miggins and neither had

Hupskin Harold or his father. The three of them had drunk Miss Margaret's sassafras tea and fled the scene long before Old Man Miggins and his posse showed up.

There was a wood sign behind them. The letters were faded, but Miggins had no trouble deciphering it: "Copper Canyon. Elevation 600 meters."

"I'll be damned," Miggins said out loud and then quietly to himself, "so that's where they jumped up and ran off to so many years ago. They came here, to live with the *Rarámuri* side of Tunis's hybrid family." Miggins didn't bother wondering why Hupskin and his father decided to stay. He had other things on his mind and he felt a scheme bubbling up inside him. He and the Rarámuri could join forces and manufacture a new team with each player 5.3 parts *Rarámuri* and whatever-the-hell else they decided. This would be the fastest team ever.

"Good day sirs," Miggins said, trying to remain calm, but the site of Tunis moving so graceful was too much.

"Hey son, did ya ever play any baseball? I know this league, not too far from here either. They're looking for pla..."

Before Old Man Miggins could finish his sentence, Tunis, Hupskin Harold, and his father sprinted towards the canyon. Miggins was left in a cloud of dusty exhaust. He took a swig of wine and toasted Gregory Sanara and proceeded to do the same for every LOF player who perished in the crash. In a matter of minutes he was good and drunk so he took a deep breath and swigged some more, toasting all LOF players yet to be.

He dreamed up outfielder Damien Office, a hybrid mix of NASCAR pit crew and Mohawk ironworker. Miggins took another swig and dreamed up second baseman Dirk Flippert, a tribreed mix of West African Fulani storyteller, union organizer, and fastidious stamp collector.

Miggins leaned against a tree and slumped slowly to the ground, passing  out just as the stars began to fill up the sky.

# Expos Next Generation

Charles A. Morris burrowed away during Montreal winters and come spring discovered all over again that snow couldn't keep it together. It turned to water and gushed down the mountainside with no need for directions.

Charles never wondered why. He removed his animal furs and enjoyed the nakedness, ate french fries and cheese curds mixed with gravy at outdoor cafes. Even in March when spring was barely on anyone's radar and snow was still falling, Charlie felt a change coming and it often overwhelmed him, turned him into a runaway train.

March of 2014 was no different. Winter was being its regular stubborn snail, taking its sweet ol' time to pass the baton to spring and Charlie surrendered nearly all of his worldly possessions, keeping only a quilt, a lamp, and a teapot. Some said it was cabin fever that impaired his judgment. Others weren't so generous.

"Are you out of your mind?" asked his youngest daughter Melissa. "Where's your winter coat and the spice rack I bought you for Christmas? Where did it all go? Even the TV is gone!"

Melissa took a few deep breaths, but couldn't shake the aggravation. She pointed her finger and screamed. "Charles A. Morris. What the hell is a matter with you?"

Charles didn't budge. He'd heard the sound of her screams a thousand times before.

"Take a look at the quilt, sweetheart," Charlie pleaded. "Beautiful, isn't it? And how about that lamp and the tea pot? Gifts from the neighbor I guess. They must have thought I was moving." Charlie snapped his fingers and tried to do a little dance, but his hips didn't cooperate. He smiled just the same.

He had given away everything, from wide lapel suits to an envelope opener, orange juice strainer, kitchen table, knives and forks, and whatever he couldn't get rid of, he dropped at the Salvation Army door. The desire to free his life of things came on suddenly, like a strange virus. He spread out items on the front lawn of his east end Montreal apartment complex and waited for the pack rats and collectors.

There was no need to post fliers on light posts because The Toronto Blue Jays and New York Mets were scheduled to play two exhibition games in Montreal that weekend and Charlie's neighborhood was already abuzz. He lived less than three blocks from Olympic Stadium—the Big O, former home of the Expos.

There hadn't been a big league game in Montreal since Sept, 29, 2004, when Termel Sledge popped out to third base to end a 9-1 loss to the Florida Marlins. That was over 10 years ago. And almost every night since then, Charlie walked the short block-and-a-half to Pascal's bar and grill, sat at the rail and talked Expos with strangers whether they wanted to or not. Every bartender was given specific instructions.

"Give him (Charlie) a Stoneman and a pitcher of beer."

Stoneman was Bill Stoneman, the only Expos pitcher to throw two no-hitters, the first one a mere three weeks into the inaugural 1969 Expos season, and beer was beer, designed to raise Charlie's Expos fever even higher.

Pascal would often play the original audio broadcast of Stoneman's April 17, 1969 no-hitter or any regular season game he could get a hold of. It never felt like nostalgia to Charlie, more like a time machine with plastic horn vuvuzelas echoing from speakers and into the bar. Pascal enhanced the situation by steaming hot dogs at the back of the bar. Sometimes kids barely old enough to drink found themselves stuck beside Charlie at the rail.

He never noticed their hats. It was too dark inside the bar, but even with more light, Charlie would have been confused because one hat was yellow and black and another green and gray and yet all of them featured the Expo emblem. The traditional red, white and blue cap had exploded into a psychedelic hodgepodge and there were more Expos hats on Montreal heads than ever before.

"These kids today wouldn't know the difference between an Expo and an Eskimo," Charlie's drinking buddy would often say.

"You old fart," Charlie yelled. "A museum is a museum and even better when it's walking on two legs and breathing."

Charlie noticed a young man wearing a black and yellow Expos cap one night and asked,

"Do you know who the Expos drafted with their first pick?"

The young man had no idea and began to remove his cap, but as he did, Charlie gently patted it back down on his head.

"It was the expansion draft in 1968, and we snatched Manny Mota from the Pirates, who wore black and yellow hats, just like the one you're wearing." The young man asked a question about Blue Monday and then one about the Olympic Stadium roof and Bill Lee and the Brasserie. A conversation launched, another round of beers was ordered, and so on into the soon-to-be blurry night.

The memories were vines crawling up and down Charlie's spine, acupuncture jolts that brought him to life. He remembered when players worked winter jobs, rode subways to and from games, sat beside fans who said things like, "Hey Mack, why'd you go and swing at that pitch?"

Charlie sat and wondered what was next for Montreal, if anything at all, but he was happy just the same, with beer in his belly. Maybe the Expos' new home, Washington D.C., thinks Mack Jones is a truck and that's OK. That's better than OK, Charlie thought, because whoever doesn't know will soon discover it for the first time.

It was a crisp March morning when Melissa dropped by and learned what her father had done. After her initial outburst, she took a deep breath and reached for her Smart phone, playing pen pal with someone in cyberspace. Charlie imagined walking across Quebec, Newfoundland, and Nova Scotia spreading Expos joy. He announced his plans to Melissa as "a pilgrimage that must be done."

Melissa didn't look up. She continued punching keys and so Charlie repeated the bit about a pilgrimage and added, "I must do it."

"Must do what! What in God's name are you talking about?"

"A pilgrimage," Charlie repeated and nodded his head slowly, up and down.

Melissa was more scared than angry, scared of Alzheimer's, a brain tumor, or latent Schizophrenia. Her father's apartment was completely empty other than the quilt, lamp, and teapot and he was talking out of his mind.

Melissa also found some folded up papers that turned out to be maps of Quebec, but not the mass production colorful kind. These were homemade sketches Charlie had made in pencil, a dozen or more maps of actual caravan routes taken by old Expos teams during the off season, back when players barnstormed into small Quebec towns to meet their fans who would then journey to Montreal from Abitibi, Thetford Mines, St.-Jean-sur-Richelieu and as far away as Edmundston, New Brunswick and Halifax, Nova Scotia. The Expos were more than Montreal or Quebec's team. They were Canada's team for nearly 10 years before the Toronto Blue Jays existed.

Charlie was a third-generation Scotsman, but spoke a decent Quebec French, and he had baseball to thank for that. The team had no name in 1968, no logo, no players, no stadium, no uniforms, and roughly 200 days to figure it all out, but French Canada knew something about baseball. The Quebec Provincial Leagues played in the late 19th century and the AAA Montreal Royals were the top farm team for the Brooklyn Dodgers until the early 1960's.

The language of baseball had been integrated into French, but the announcement that a MLB team was coming sent broadcasters and journalists into a pleasant frenzy, to make expressions official, so fans could share a common baseball language.

Charlie was 23 years young when he attended his first baseball game at Jarry Park. It was August 6, 1969. He may have given away all of his worldy possessions, but not the ticket stub from that day. He sat behind home plate and watched future Hall of Famer Phil Niekro strike out nine Expos and win 6-3, but it wasn't the strikeouts or Niekro's complete game that Charlie remembered. It was a French word fans sitting next to him kept repeating: *papillon, papillon, papillon*. Charlie had heard it before, in high school French class, and he knew it meant "butterfly," but in baseball? He stared at the mound and watched the ball sail from Niekro's fingertip grip, darting and diving every which way. Those fans were right; it was *une balle papillon* – a butterfly ball. Knuckles had nothing to do with it.

And in the ninth inning of that same game with the Expos trailing 6-2, Rusty Staub stepped to the plate and he hit one high and deep that sailed over the wall for a home run, but that's not what Charlie remembered. When Staub ran out to right field in the next half inning, those same fans referred to him as *le voltigeur de droite*. *Charlie* scribbled some semblance of the word *voltigeur* onto his program. He had heard the word before and later that evening dug out his French dictionary. He discovered that *voltigeur* comes from the word "vault" and dates back to soldiers leaping onto the backs of horses during the Napoleonic Wars.

Charlie never bothered memorizing the gender of French nouns, but baseball made learning the language much more enjoyable, and 45 years later, Charlie could have used a horse to vault on to flee from his daughter who had a not-so-loving look on her face. She handed Charlie the folder filled with the caravan maps.

"You've been planning this for a while, haven't you?" Melissa asked. "And you never told me! We could have rented a Winnebago."

Charlie didn't catch the sarcasm, or if he did, he played eye for an eye. "What a brilliant idea! A caravan of Expos fans."

And then he yelled, "My daughter the genius! Why didn't I think of that! I'll raise you one and instead of a Winnebago, we'll paddle canoes, beginning in Montreal and zigzag our way north and east along the St. Lawrence River and people will recognize the Expos emblem painted on the side of our canoe."

"Don't forget the Mississippi River, New Orleans, and the Acadian descendants," said Melissa with a convincing smile.

"Yes, of course," Charlie yelled. "There's bound to be Rusty Staub fans in the Bayou. Maybe you're right, Melissa. Maybe we should go with the Winnebago, or better yet, we can strap a canoe on top and switch back and forth. We're gonna need to rest our arms from all that paddling, especially us older ones. We can do more of the driving."

Melissa nodded her head in agreement. She was trying to gain her father's trust by feigning interest in the Expos.

"What letters make up the Expos logo?" Melissa asked, while leading her father by the arm outside.

Charlie never had a chance to answer. Short pudgy fingers squeezed his neck and shoulder blade. A blindfold was wrapped over his eyes and he was stuffed into the back of a van.

"This is 2003 all over again," Charlie screamed while gasping for breath. "You hijacked the Expos and forced them to play home games in San Juan, Puerto Rico, 2,000 miles away, and now you're hijacking me. Let me out of here!"

SLAM! The doors of the van shut and the lock clicked. There were no windows. The driver revved the engine and bumped through space and time, and so did Charlie. He pounded the door a few times, but the bouncing was too much. He sat down and remembered the Expos being in the wild card race back in 2003. It was September, time to expand the 25-man rosters to

40, add prospects and veterans for the final push, but not the Expos, not in 2003 because their free will was snatched "just like mine!" Charlie screamed.

The details flashed like headlines in his mind. Expos told *"no money to call up players. Your roster stays at 25"* and so it did and the Expos went 12-15 in September and faded away, eight games behind the wild card, and the following season, they faded even further, out of town and country, to Washington DC to become the Nationals.

Charlie must have fallen asleep, because when he woke up he was no longer in the back of a van. He was sleeping very comfortably in a bed with clean crisp sheets, but couldn't move to the right or left. And when he tried to sit up, he suffered a whiplash sensation throwing him back to the bed. Melissa greeted him with a big smile. Charlie was the first to speak.

"Let me out of here. Where did they take us?"

Melissa lowered her head onto Charlie's stomach and smothered the sound of her pretend sobs. She was the one who sent text messages to The Holtzman Center, in order to "rescue her father from fanaticism."

The Center was run by Hasidic Jews. Charlie was not Jewish. No one in his family was and that's exactly why Melissa selected Holtzman. She believed a new environment would steer Charlie's thinking away from the Expos.

Each patient was assigned a study partner to partake in one-on-one discussions and debates. The method known as *chavrusa*, or friendship, was modeled after young boys studying Hebrew texts. They become so engaged in the activity that all other interests fade away.

Charlie was matched with a **23**-year old whose mission was to transfer Charlie's Expos fanaticism onto another team, one still in existence.

The lights were turned off and Charlie did exactly what the Holtzman Center hoped he would do. He complained, and so the lights were turned back on, but very slowly, and accompanied by the sound of Fernand Lapierre's Jarry Park organ playing softly from the speakers.

*"Mets ton jolie chapeau. Je t'emmènes voir les Expos." Put on your lovely hat. I'm taking you to see the Expos."*

Charlie didn't remember all the words but he hummed along until the needle made its last ka-kshhhh on the turntable hidden somewhere in the wall.

"Let's read something" were the first words Yonkel Schwartz spoke to Charlie. No "good morning, my name is," no handshakes or joking around, just "Let's read something." And so they did.

Yonkel reached under the bed and tinkered with a few buttons as if he were hot wiring a car. The side rails of the bed dropped and Charlie was free to move about the room and sit at the table and so he did. Yonkel slid a few pages towards him and began to read a story about a rabbi who asked *a student his favorite Hebrew letter. The student said, "Aleph-* א *because it looks like the New York Yankees logo with the Y on top of the N."*

*The rabbi smiled and discussed the birth of the letter Aleph thousands of years ago and how it's the same letter "we read today." His student changed the subject to the birth of the Yankees logo in 1913 and said, "It's the same one the Yankees use today, from Babe Ruth to Joe DiMaggio to Mickey Mantle, tradition, tradition, tradition."*

*And 20 years later, that same student/Yankees fan became a rabbi himself and when he asked his student his favorite Hebrew letter, lo and behold, the student said, "Aleph- א because it looks like the New York Yankees logo, the Y on top of the N," adding "Thurman Munson, Bernie Williams, and Derek Jeter to the tradition, tradition, tradition."*

Charlie was well aware of the medication this hospital or rehab center was slipping him. He never swallowed a damn thing and realized right away that Yonkel Schwartz and his Yankees story and all this talk of tradition tradition tradition were attempts to hijack Charlie's mind and extinguish his Expos passion. Charlie put on his best poker face, determined to out-trick the tricksters without arousing any suspicion.

Charlie knew not to eat a damn thing, not even drink the water. He had seen enough movies to know how these prisoner of war situations turn out. He stuffed all food and medication in his pocket and smuggled it to the toilet for a ritual flushing.

Activities at the center shut down from Friday to Saturday sundown in religious observance of Shabbat, and lucky for Charlie, his first day was Friday—a perfect time to escape. He waited until sunset and folded a sheet over his head to resemble a prayer shawl like others were wearing. He slipped quietly down a flight of stairs and exited the building. He walked through unfamiliar streets until he reached a playground and rested inside a sand box. "A perfect place to get some sleep, just like the beach," Charlie mumbled to himself. "Soft on the back and beautiful under the stars."

He awoke with the sun and immediately recognized where he was—a few blocks from Kemzin Park. There was a scoreboard in right center, but most of the bulbs for balls, strikes, and outs were broken or missing. Charlie scanned the infield and his mind flashed back to 1976 and kids hopping on sting ray bikes riding east along Ducharme and then north up St. Laurent Street towards Jarry Park for a swim and the Expos hosting the San Diego Padres.

And then his mind flashed back even further, to 1946 and kids riding bikes south and east towards Delorimier Stadium where the Montreal Royals are playing the Syracuse Chiefs and Jackie Robinson is enjoying a .468 OB% during his only season in Montreal.

And now it was Charlie's turn. He walked 10 minutes to the Plamondon subway station, boarded the orange line, transferred to an eastbound green line and arrived at Olympic Stadium in 38 minutes.

The subway doors swished open and a rumble began in Charlie's stomach. He walked through the underground tunnel connecting the subway to Olympic Stadium. Pictures of Expos players no longer lined the walls, but Charlie knew that already. He had walked through this very tunnel dozens of times since the Expos left Montreal and it never bothered him before, but now he struggled to breathe. He managed to reach the main concourse where he heard that familiar sound of "Get your scorecards and programs here," but there were Blue Jays on the cover and Charlie felt a sudden emptiness in his stomach.

"Why do I have to meet you again?" Charlie asked, not realizing it would be so difficult to enter Olympic Stadium without the Expos. He took slow breaths and reminded himself that there was going to be a celebration inside with players from the 1994 Expos introduced, but he still couldn't pass through the turnstiles, not yet anyway.

He already had his ticket so he walked outside and up the hill, towards Sherbrooke Street in search of a distraction. Maybe the Appalachian mountains or shipping cranes along the St. Lawrence River would get his mind right. The water spread in both directions, to the Great Lakes in the west and Atlantic Ocean in the East, but Charlie looked at a stranger a few feet in front of him instead. He was wearing a Minnesota Twins backpack. A good omen, Charlie thought. Minnesota was once without a team. Charlie popped the obvious question, "You traveled all the way from Minnesota just to see a game at Olympic Stadium?"

"I grew up in Minnesota," the stranger said, "Now I live in New Jerseay. But yes, I came to see Olympic Stadium."

"I never bump into Twins fans around here," Charlie said, "Only Red Sox and Yankee fanatics. I prefer the M in Minnesota. It's like the M in Montreal."

The stranger laughed. He'd been to all 30 MLB parks, but not Olympic Stadium.

Their conversation seesawed back and forth, from the Boston Braves to Tim Raines, Harvey Haddix, and baseball's first official statistician, Allan Roth being from Montreal. There was no end in sight. Charlie looked towards the river, amazed how two complete strangers instantly became long-lost baseball buddies. All part of the caravan. He was ready to try again.

They walked towards the stadium. Charlie took a deep breath and slipped through the turnstiles. It was like riding a bike all over again. He led the way towards what used to be the Expos dugout and they watched the Mets take batting practice.

Brandon Marrow pitched superb for the Blue Jays and Melky Cabrera hit a two-run homer in the bottom of the eighth. The Blue Jays won, but fans chanted, "Let's go Expos, Let's go Expos."

As the crowd made its way for the exits, including Charlie and his new friend, that empty feeling in Charlie's stomach returned.

Charlie's life flashed before his eyes, or a 36-year Expos history did anyway, from scrambling for a name and a place to play in 1968 to a standing room only crowd at Jarry Park and the dugout fiddler, Fernand La Pierre's organ, Jonesville and Staub, the swimming pool beyond right field, and then the move to Olympic Stadium—The Big O. and the clack and echo of seats as fans lifted them up and down, followed by those tragic words of the young ushers, "time to go home folks."

Charlie strolled a while among the Expos fans and then made his way to Pascal's Pub for what he hoped would be a spillover crowd from the game, but all went dark instead and a blindfold was wrapped over his eyes and once again he was stuffed into a van.

"This is just like 1994," Charlie screamed. "On a roll, best record in baseball and a strike ends the seas...."

Charlie couldn't finish the sentence. The doors opened. It was Melissa. She jumped into the van and removed the blindfold and instantly became more than Charlie's daughter. She became a hero and savior.

Melissa's plan didn't play out exactly as she had hoped. Charlie had escaped, but when the Holtzman center phoned, Melissa wasn't worried. She knew exactly where he would be.

The Blue Jays-Mets game was scheduled for that very afternoon and so she took over the operation, going first to Pascal's bar where she hatched a new strategy with Charlie's friends.

She then instructed the Holtzman Rehab Center driver to park the van beside Pascal's and wait. And when Charlie approached after the game, she winked, a signal "to get to work, to apprehend her father." Three men then exited the van. And when the deed was done, Melissa nodded her head and said, "Thank you very much. I'll take it from here." She could now be the liberator, rescuer or whatever Charlie might imagine. What mattered most was that, from then on, she could pull his strings in whatever ways she deemed necessary.

Melissa put her arm around Charlie's waist and escorted him towards her car. They drove in the opposite direction of Olympic Stadium, away from Charlie's vacant apartment.

"So what does the Expos emblem stand for?" Melissa asked. "You never did tell me."

Charlie was still talking when they reached Melissa's house. He walked around to the driver's side and opened the door and helped his daughter to a standing position and together they waltzed, hand-in-hand, to the front step and sat down. Charlie had more to say about the Expos logo.

"An e, M and b for Expos Montreal baseball," Charlie explained. "A curvy, fleur-de-lys **M** for **M**ontreal, an **e**, *l*, b for **E**xpos **l**eague **b**aseball and **e**skimos **l**ove **b**aseball, **c** and **b** to honor Expos owner **C**harles **B**ronfman, and so on and so forth and there will be so many more." Charlie waited a few seconds, smiled and said very slowly; "c-a-r-a-v-a-n."

Melissa walked Charlie to the atrium in the back of her house where Expos pennants and posters covered the walls and three of Charlie's drinking buddies were seated around a table. The peach lamp was in the middle and turquoise teapot and four cups surrounded it. The blanket was folded up and laying at the edge of a couch. A radio broadcast of an old Expos game played in the background.

"What season are we in?" asked one of his friends.

Another friend offered a hint, "Pedro Martinez wasn't even born."

Charlie turned around and hugged his daughter.

"It's all yours Daddy, and with warm summer temperatures, we'll remove the roof and side panels, make an open air patio garden."

"A retractable roof," insisted Charlie.

"We'll build a sculpture of Staub," said the third friend.

Melissa had corralled her father and attached him to an invisible leash. She was satisfied. The caravan and pilgrimage had been contained inside her own house, but there was already talk in Montreal of making the exhibition game an annual event.